COURTING THE EARL

LANDING A LORD

SUZANNA MEDEIROS

COURTING THE EARL

Eleanor Pearson is distressed by the forbidden attraction she feels for her cousin's betrothed. But she vows to ignore her fascination with the attractive earl and do whatever she can to ensure her cousin's marriage takes place.

The Earl of Hargrove has no intention of marrying anytime soon. He sets out on a mission of his own to end the surprise arrangement his father revealed to him only on his deathbed.

It doesn't take him long to realize that Eleanor could be the key to convincing the younger woman to end the betrothal. But his attraction to her threatens his determination to remain a bachelor.

To learn about Suzanna Medeiros's future books, you can sign up for her newsletter at https://www. suzannamedeiros.com/newsletter.

CHAPTER 1

February 1818

Eleanor Pearson stepped into a pale yellow muslin gown and turned so her aunt's maid could fasten the short row of buttons.

It was not yet noon, too early to be preparing to receive callers, but this morning's guest was special. The Earl of Hargrove would soon arrive to meet with her uncle. Of course Aunt Helen wouldn't allow this opportunity to pass. The earl was formally betrothed to her daughter Lydia, but the two had yet to meet.

In truth, none of them had met the new earl. Eleanor couldn't deny she was very curious about the man who would be marrying her cousin.

"Your hair, Miss Pearson?"

Eleanor turned to face the maid. They both knew the woman should be concentrating on Lydia. "I can manage. You should see to my cousin."

With a quick curtsy, the woman left the room.

Eleanor sat at the dressing table and frowned at her appearance. Yellow was not a good color on her as it gave her fair skin a sallow appearance. She'd chosen to wear this dress today for precisely that reason.

She pinned her brown hair up in a practical chignon, careful to scrape it back tightly. Today was all about Lydia, and Eleanor had been admonished by her aunt not to do anything to overshadow her younger cousin.

As though that were possible. No one would notice Eleanor while Lydia was in the room.

Her movements were quick and efficient since she knew what was coming. She'd just set down her hairbrush when a piercing shriek rang out through the house. Eleanor rose from the dressing table and waited for the inevitable summons.

"Ellie!"

With a sigh, she smoothed her hands over her dress and made her way down the hall to her cousin's chamber. The scene that greeted her was less chaotic than she'd feared.

Lydia sat on the edge of her bed, three gowns cast aside behind her. A fourth dress was draped over the maid's arm. No doubt the woman had deemed it safer to hold on to it rather than risk Lydia tossing that one aside as well.

Eleanor crossed the room to stand before Lydia, who reached for her hands and clutched them.

"What am I going to do? All these dresses were made last year. The new ones we ordered from the modiste haven't arrived yet."

Eleanor squeezed Lydia's hands. "Let me see if I can find something special."

She turned to Lydia's wardrobe and began to look through the many dresses hanging there. Her cousin already possessed a number of beautiful gowns made with rich fabrics, but it was true that she didn't have many day dresses.

Finally she settled on a white morning dress with blue lace trim around the bodice and sleeves.

She turned to Lydia, holding the dress out. "I've always loved this one on you. The blue trim matches your eyes and makes them look larger."

A crease formed between Lydia's brows. "But it isn't new."

"No, but Lord Hargrove has never seen you in it. Besides, he is a man. Such things don't matter to him. He'll just see a beautiful young woman and will become besotted at once."

A dimple formed in Lydia's cheek, because of course her cousin also had dimples. Eleanor wasn't similarly blessed.

"What would I do without you, Ellie?"

Eleanor lowered herself onto the bed beside her cousin. Lydia was spoiled, yes, but she wasn't mean-spirited. It wasn't Lydia's fault that her parents had always indulged her every whim.

"You'll never have to find out. Now let's get you ready to meet your betrothed."

THEY MADE THEIR WAY DOWNSTAIRS HALF AN HOUR later, after Lydia was satisfied with the way her fair hair framed her heart-shaped face. Aunt Helen was already sitting in the drawing room, reading what Eleanor suspected was a scandal sheet. They'd only been in London two days, but her aunt always loved staying abreast of the latest scandals and on-dit.

Eleanor greeted her aunt with a kiss to her

cheek and moved to the settee, watching as Lydia did the same before coming to sit next to her.

Lady Appleby tsked. "The early hour is most inconvenient. I had to cancel an appointment with the modiste."

Lydia pouted. "Is Lord Hargrove expected soon?"

Eleanor picked up the small basket one of the maids had brought down earlier so she could continue to work on her embroidery. While she wasn't a fan of tagging along with her aunt and cousin as they continued with their unspoken mission of visiting every modiste on Bond Street, she liked embroidery even less. But it kept her thoughts partially occupied as the pair went over the long list of items they wanted to purchase for Lydia's upcoming season. It seemed that the list kept growing longer. They'd been in town for two days now and had spent most of that time shopping.

She supposed it was a good thing her uncle was wealthy. Heaven knew Lady Appleby would be content to purchase the world for her only child.

The two discussed returning to the modiste that afternoon to order even more dresses. It was almost identical to the conversation they'd had yesterday, only then they'd been discussing milliners.

"I don't know why you're wearing that horrid dress. It makes you look quite ill."

Eleanor wasn't really paying attention to the conversation, and so it took her a few seconds to realize the comment had been addressed to her.

She looked up to find Lydia frowning at her.

Eleanor lifted one shoulder in a casual shrug. "It doesn't matter what I'm wearing. Lord Hargrove is coming here to see you and not me."

Lydia arched one brow. "You're coming with us when we go shopping."

Eleanor held back her wince. "Aunt and Uncle have already been very generous with me. I'm sure my wardrobe will suffice for those occasions when I'm called upon to act as your chaperone in Aunt Helen's absence."

"I insist," Lydia said with a shake of her head. "This might be your last chance to find a husband. Just because I'm already betrothed doesn't mean the two of us can't enjoy the season."

Lydia's generosity was only one of the reasons Eleanor loved her cousin so much. It was true that Lydia was spoiled, but she wasn't selfish.

"Of course I'll come with you. But truly I don't

need anything. I'm quite content with the dresses in my wardrobe."

"Well, we'll need to find one to replace that ghastly thing because I plan to burn it later. Honestly, how is it possible that you can help me choose the perfect dress this morning but decide to wear that?"

Eleanor had no reply to Lydia's criticism. Her cousin was exactly right, but the last thing she wanted was Aunt Helen thinking she was trying to overshadow her cousin. It wouldn't be possible of course, but still. She was very aware that she was at the mercy of her father's brother and his wife. They'd always been kind to Eleanor, but it was very clear that their world revolved around Lydia. She didn't want to behave in any way that might lead to their censure.

A knock sounded then, unnaturally loud. Eleanor set her embroidery down on her lap and waited. She glanced at Lydia, who smiled back at her with a wide grin.

"Patience," Aunt Helen murmured.

"Yes, Mama," Lydia said before taking a few deep breaths and working to keep her expression even.

When she heard the deep voice of a man

speaking to their butler, Eleanor was surprised at the nerves that fluttered to life in her belly. She attributed it to concern for Lydia.

And then her cousin's betrothed stepped into the room.

Aunt Helen stood to greet him and dipped into a curtsy. "It is a pleasure to make your acquaintance, my lord. I know Lord Appleby reached out to you last year, but I was sorry to hear about your father's passing and wanted to extend my condolences personally."

Eleanor tried not to stare, but she couldn't help but be taken aback by the man's appearance. He was quite tall. Light brown hair was brushed back from his face, and when his gaze made a quick survey of the room and its occupants, she noticed his eyes were an attractive shade of blue.

"Thank you," he said with a small bow. "It is a pleasure to make your acquaintance."

His bow was executed with a casual elegance, and Eleanor had to hold back a sigh. Heavens, Lord Hargrove and Lydia would make beautiful babies.

Aunt Helen turned toward the settee. "Allow me to introduce my daughter, Lydia Pearson."

Lydia stood and dipped into a flawless curtsy.

Eleanor was content to watch the scene play out

from her seat on the settee. This was the part where Lord Hargrove would flush, perhaps even stammer, as he gazed upon the woman who was to be his bride. Instead, he murmured a smooth "A pleasure" and then turned to look at Eleanor.

There was a tense moment where Eleanor felt her heart trip in her chest under his scrutiny.

Finally her aunt gave a small laugh. "Oh, and this is my niece, Miss Eleanor Pearson."

Eleanor stood and dipped into her own curtsy. "My lord." She hadn't expected to be a participant in the morning's tableau.

He said nothing more. Just as the moment began to stretch into awkwardness, Aunt Helen spoke. "Let me call for refreshments—"

"It is a pleasure to meet all of you, but since we haven't been properly introduced, I should speak to Lord Appleby first."

"Oh, of course." Aunt Helen's hand fluttered to her chest. "Silly me, I got carried away since you'll soon be part of the family. My husband is in his study and is expecting you."

Eleanor thought she saw his jaw clench at Aunt Helen's words, but that must have been her imagination. After meeting Lydia, Lord Hargrove was no doubt overjoyed by the prospect of his upcoming marriage.

Aunt Helen summoned the footman who was waiting in the hallway and instructed him to show their guest to Uncle's study.

Silence descended after the man left, the only sound the echo of fading footsteps. Finally they heard the murmur of male voices and then the study door closing.

When no one spoke, Eleanor sat and took up her embroidery again. "He has impeccable manners." She wanted to comment on his good looks as well but refrained.

Aunt Helen let out a soft sniff of annoyance and returned to her seat. "Yes, he has every-thing we could want in a suitable match. Title, breeding, no hint of a scandal. And he's attrac-tive enough for dear Lydia. Not that one should base these decisions on appearance, but it does help."

Eleanor had no doubt that her aunt was thinking about her future grandchildren, who would all be beautiful.

Lydia dropped onto the settee next to her. "He's so old."

Eleanor's mouth dropped open, but she caught

herself and quickly closed it again. "Unless I'm mistaken, he's not yet thirty."

Lydia let out a heavy sigh. "I suppose he doesn't seem old to you, but I'm only eighteen."

Eleanor was only twenty-five, so it wasn't as though she was ancient herself. Still, society had a different set of rules for men and women. No one thought anything of much older men marrying young women, yet Eleanor would be considered by many to already be on the shelf. The double standard bothered her more than she cared to admit.

Lydia folded her arms over her waist and settled back into the cushions. "He barely looked at me."

Eleanor had known that was what really bothered her cousin. Truth be told, Eleanor had been surprised as well. She could only attribute it to the fact that Lord Hargrove was no doubt a man of the world. He probably met beautiful young women every spring when society descended on London for the social season. In their neighboring village back home at their country estate, Lydia always caused a sensation. Still, Eleanor couldn't deny that his lack of a noticeable reaction had been unexpected.

They'd yet to attend their first ball, but they'd all assumed Lydia would be the diamond of the season. Eleanor couldn't be sure how her cousin would react if that turned out not to be true. If nothing else, it could be a character-building lesson in showing the young woman that the world did not, in fact, revolve around her.

She patted Lydia's knee. "I'm sure it's as he said. He just wanted to meet with Uncle first. Despite the fact the betrothal arrangements have been in place for several years, I have no doubt he's in the study right now, asking for permission to court you."

Lydia frowned, a small vee forming between her brows. "I'm going to make him wait."

"You're already betrothed," Aunt Helen said.

"If this is to be my only season, I want to experience it fully. Papa has already agreed."

Her aunt tried again. "But the agreement—"

Lydia shook her head. "That doesn't mean he shouldn't have to pursue me."

It was times like these when it was almost painfully obvious to Eleanor just how young her cousin was. Perhaps it would be good if Lydia wasn't the most sought-after young woman that season.

Eleanor had already learned that life didn't always work out the way one expected it to when first her mother, then her father, died while she was still young. Lydia, by contrast, had always had the world handed to her.

She didn't wish ill on Lydia, and Eleanor was very aware of the fact that she was one of the people who went out of their way to shelter her cousin. But she couldn't help fearing that Lord Hargrove might not be content to dance attendance on Lydia.

She refused to consider that possibility. No, everything would work out as they'd all hoped this season.

CHAPTER 2

Geoffrey bowed his head and took his leave, chafing under the intense scrutiny of the three women as he followed the footman from the room. He shouldn't have been surprised to find them waiting for him, yet he was.

When he'd sent a note to Lord Appleby yesterday to set up today's meeting, he'd thought his intentions were clear. He wanted to discuss the betrothal agreement with the viscount, not walk into a room filled with women who'd stared at him with curious, breathless anticipation. Had they expected him to fall prostrate at the feet of Miss Pearson?

He should have asked Appleby to meet him

elsewhere and wouldn't make the same mistake in future.

Pushing aside his annoyance, Geoffrey brought his thoughts back to the task at hand—convincing Lord Appleby to call off the betrothal.

His mouth firmed. It was galling that his father had made these arrangements without consulting him ten years ago. He'd been nineteen, not yet at his age of majority but still too damn old to be kept in the dark about what his father was doing.

The fact that he'd kept it a secret, that he'd only revealed the truth on his deathbed, meant the man had known Geoffrey would be angry. Furious. Feeling his temper start to rise again, he took a deep breath and tried to regain his composure.

The footman stopped before a closed door—the study, he presumed—and knocked softly. At least Appleby had given instructions that Geoffrey was to be admitted instead of forcing him to wait in the drawing room with the women.

The door was opened moments later by Lord Appleby.

They'd met briefly years ago during one of Geoffrey's holidays from university. Was that when the two older men had finalized the marriage arrangements? Had Appleby insisted on meeting him first to ensure he was suitable?

Appleby shook his hand in welcome. "Thank you for calling today. We have only just arrived in town, and I'd hoped to reach out to you soon."

Geoffrey watched him close the door, offering them privacy for their conversation. "I wasn't expecting to make a formal call today."

Appleby shook his head. "I must apologize for my wife's enthusiasm. When she heard about your visit, she insisted on greeting you personally."

"And you didn't want to be there to introduce us?"

Lord Appleby shrugged. "I'm afraid time got away from me."

Geoffrey gritted his teeth at the viscount's insincere apology.

Lord Appleby indicated the two chairs that were nestled into one corner of the study. When they were seated, the man's expectant gaze settled on Geoffrey's face.

"You met my daughter?"

Geoffrey inclined his head. "Yes, as well as your niece."

"And?"

"She seems to be a pleasant young woman."

Appleby frowned. "Pleasant? She's going to be the most sought-after young woman this season. Many hopes—and I daresay hearts—will break when your betrothal is announced."

Geoffrey tried to keep his expression impassive. "That's why I'm here to see you."

Appleby chuckled. "I understand. Now that you've met Lydia, I'm sure you want to speak to me about having the wedding as soon as possible. But I must inform you that I promised her we'd wait until the end of the season to announce the betrothal. It's her first season, and she wants to enjoy the months ahead."

Geoffrey examined the man in front of him, hope beginning to take hold. The viscount was so different from his own parent. Father would have been champing at the bit to seal the deal to ensure his plans were carried out. The fact that Lord Appleby seemed more concerned about his daughter's happiness led Geoffrey to feel optimism for the first time since learning of the agreement.

"It is obvious that you care very much about your daughter."

A smile lit Appleby's face. "She is everything to her mother and me. I know she'll far exceed your expectations as the Countess Hargrove."

"But not before she enjoys a measure of freedom first."

Appleby brushed aside the words. "It is her first season, and surely there is no hurry. I understand your disappointment. We'll have a large affair at the end of the season instead of rushing things now. We wouldn't want anyone to whisper about unseemly haste."

Geoffrey kept his tone as even as possible. "It's possible that in the coming months, she might find that she doesn't want to be my countess. That she'd rather accept one of the other men who will want to court her."

Geoffrey might be stubborn, but he wasn't blind. Lydia Pearson was beautiful. Her father wasn't exaggerating in assuming that many men would be clamoring for her attention.

Appleby's smile widened. "Then you'll have to ensure her attention doesn't stray. I'm sure a fine young man like yourself won't find the task onerous."

Geoffrey hesitated a moment before saying, "And if I feel that we don't suit?"

Appleby's smile dimmed as he stared at Geoffrey for several seconds. It was as though he couldn't comprehend his statement. "I don't understand."

"I mean no offense, my lord. It is just that I am only twenty-nine years of age. I hadn't expected to wed for several years yet."

Finally Appleby shook his head. "But the betrothal—"

"Can be nullified with the agreement of both parties."

The viscount's mouth drew into a straight line and he looked away. Seconds ticked by, the silence growing uncomfortable. Finally he stood. Geoffrey did the same.

Appleby's hands were clenched. "No."

"As you've said, your daughter is a delightful young woman. There are many who will seek her out. She will have her pick from any suitor she desires."

Appleby continued as though Geoffrey hadn't spoken at all. "The betrothal stands. I suggest you spend some time over the next few months getting to know your future wife."

"And if she doesn't wish to marry me?"

Appleby shook his head. "Your father and I came to an agreement. Arrangements have already been made."

"But—"

"Enough. It is too early to discuss these things. I expect you to uphold your part of the contract."

Geoffrey warred with himself, wanting to press the issue, but in the end decided now was not the time. He'd raised the possibility of breaking the betrothal. To continue right now would only cause insult, and then he might never find his way out of this marriage.

"I apologize for my bluntness. I meant no offense. I only learned of the betrothal recently."

Lord Appleby grimaced. "And you were taken aback. I understand. But once you get to know Lydia, you'll see that your father couldn't have found a better match for you."

Geoffrey said nothing further on the subject as he took his leave. He kept his gaze forward as he passed the drawing room, pretending that he didn't feel the women's eyes on him as he moved past the doorway.

Unease settled over him as he climbed into his carriage. He could just imagine Lady Appleby rushing into her husband's study to demand details about their discussion. He couldn't help but wonder if the viscount would share the reason for his visit that morning since it was clear the man was intent on maintaining the betrothal.

Still, Geoffrey had learned something important from their meeting. Lord Appleby seemed to care for his daughter a great deal. But Geoffrey knew firsthand that appearances could be deceiving. How many times had his own father behaved as though he doted on Geoffrey and his sister Abigail over the years while in the presence of others? But his primary care was for his own ambitions.

Father had forced Abigail into an unhappy marriage with an older man years ago. And now he'd arranged for Geoffrey's marriage with the same lack of concern for his son's preferences.

Geoffrey tried to ignore the niggle of guilt he felt when he thought about his sister's arranged marriage. Abigail had suffered with her own situation, married to a man old enough to be her grandfather. He couldn't imagine the horror that had awaited her in the marriage bed. At least her husband had finally had the good grace to pass away and Abigail was now happily married to another.

Lydia, on the other hand, was young and beautiful. And he was aware that his own forced union wasn't a bad one. Not really. But damnation, the very last thing he wanted was to fall in line with his father's plans.

He'd give the young woman a chance, but he doubted she'd tempt him into changing his mind. She was too delicate for his taste. When he did wed several years from now, it wouldn't be to a woman he'd feel had to be handled carefully lest she break.

He was finally free from his father's control, and he planned to enjoy himself for the next few years before turning his attention to the matter of securing an heir. He just had to ensure Lydia found him unsuitable and was able to convince her father to break the betrothal contract.

CHAPTER 3

hey waited three more days before attending their first social event of the season. The Clarington ball. Lydia had been impatient, and if she were being honest, Eleanor was as well.

It wasn't the first invitation they'd received, but it was the first ball. The Duke and Duchess of Clarington's ball had recently become known as *the* start of the social season. Aunt Helen had insisted the ball would provide the perfect backdrop to launch Lydia into society.

Eleanor had to admit, her cousin looked particularly beautiful that evening. Lydia's dress was of the palest blue, the décolletage and hem trimmed with lace. Small blue and white beads threaded through the trim, winking under the candlelight and drawing the eye to her neckline. The dress was modest of course, as was befitting a proper young lady just making her debut in society, but the effect was unmistakable.

Eleanor found her own eyes drawn to the twinkling trim. She had no doubt every man in the room would be staring not at her cousin's eyes but at her bosom.

But if they managed to draw their gazes upward, they wouldn't be let down by Lydia's beauty. Her blond hair was swept up and a riot of curls that framed her face. Large blue eyes, a small nose, and a mouth that formed a perfect little bow.

They were standing arm in arm, just behind Aunt Helen and Uncle as they waited right outside the ballroom to be announced. The loud murmur of voices drifted out to greet them, and Eleanor found her anticipation growing with each second that passed.

Eleanor leaned down to speak in Lydia's ear. "Are you nervous?"

Lydia shook her head, her blond curls bouncing. "No. I'm just glad we won't be sitting at home this evening with nothing to do." She was practically vibrating with excitement.

Eleanor had to admit her cousin's happiness was infectious. It didn't hurt that Lydia had marched into her room that evening and chosen Eleanor's gown herself. And so instead of one of the more demure dresses she'd planned to wear, Eleanor was wearing a lavender gown that was quite fetching against her dark hair. Eleanor's eyes were still brown, but overall she thought she looked pretty enough even though she was quite a bit taller than most of the women present. She'd never be the beauty her cousin was, but then most women could never attain that level of perfection.

And tonight her scalp wouldn't ache when she took down her hair. Lydia had forbidden her from wearing her hair so tightly. Instead, she sported a loose chignon and a few curls framed her face. She wasn't on a par with her cousin of course, but she felt pretty. Perhaps someone would even ask her to dance.

Finally it was their turn, and her aunt and uncle stepped into the ballroom. She and Lydia followed as the butler announced them.

Eleanor's eyes swept over the spacious room, taking in the high ceilings and candlelit chandeliers. And there were so many people. It took her several seconds to realize that all those people were staring at them. Or rather, they were all looking at Lydia. And then the whispering started.

Eleanor loved her cousin, she really did, but she couldn't help but wonder what it would be like to have even one person look at her in the same way everyone was now staring at Lydia.

CHAPTER 4

$\mathcal{U}$nlike the growing crowds of people filling the large ballroom, Geoffrey wasn't thrilled to be attending the Clarington ball. But since this was the battlefield upon which his current war would be waged, here he was. Along with what seemed to be every other member of society minus his sister and brother-in-law. Abigail was quite far into her pregnancy and went to bed early most evenings, so he'd have to face tonight on his own.

He'd considered making himself odious to Miss Lydia Pearson so the young woman would beg her father to end the betrothal but had quickly discarded that plan. If he were the only one affected by his actions, he would have no issue acting the cad to drive her away. But he needed to consider his sister. Causing a scandal would hurt her far more than it would him.

Viscount Holbrook sidled up next to him and clapped him on the shoulder. "Try not to look as though you're being led to your death."

Geoffrey scowled at him, which caused Holbrook to chuckle. He wouldn't admit as much, but he was glad he wasn't entirely alone.

By unspoken agreement, they moved off to the edge of the room. Most people were congregating closer to the entrance so they could scrutinize each new guest as they were announced.

Holbrook was busy examining the guests who were already present. "Tell me about this young woman you'll be marrying."

Geoffrey clasped his hands behind his back. Of course Holbrook knew about that. The man seemed to know everything. Since an announcement wouldn't be made until the end of the season, he must have heard about the betrothal from Abigail.

He scanned the ballroom again. He hadn't heard Appleby's family being announced, but then he hadn't really been paying attention as the butler droned on with the seemingly unending list of guests. He hadn't been there long, and he was already tempted to escape to the card room.

"Did my sister send you here to keep an eye on me?"

Holbrook chuckled. "Believe it or not, it was her husband."

Geoffrey had a hard time imagining that conversation. Holbrook seemed to go out of his way to annoy Geoffrey's brother-in-law, flirting with Abigail outrageously whenever Cranston was present.

"I'm amazed he even speaks to you."

Holbrook shrugged. "We've come to an understanding. And most importantly, he loves and trusts his wife. Even if I wanted to try my hand at tempting her away…"

Geoffrey scowled at the man.

One corner of Holbrook's mouth quirked up. "I consider your sister a friend, nothing more. I had a duty to look out for her when my bastard of a great-uncle died and left his widow with very little to provide for herself and her daughter."

"That's not how Cranston tells the story of your *friendship*."

Holbrook chuckled. "Cranston was being willfully stubborn about his wife. Everyone but her could see he was obsessed with her. I did what I could to make him realize that he had to stop pushing her away."

Geoffrey could just imagine how that went. "I'm surprised the man didn't call you out."

Holbrook winced. "Would you believe that I sought him out and threatened to call him out if he hurt your sister? This was before they were married of course."

Geoffrey couldn't hold back a bark of laughter. How had he never heard this story? "My brother-in-law is a crack shot. He would have killed you."

Holbrook rubbed a hand over his jaw. "I realize now that I came perilously close to meeting my death after issuing that threat. But that's all in the past. We've reached a truce. He loves your sister, and he realizes now that my interest in her was never romantic. Which is why he told me about your situation."

Geoffrey's jaw clenched, and his eyes darted to one of the exits he'd made a point of noting after arriving. He could still slip out to the card room.

Holbrook moved in front of him. "Tell me you're not planning to cause a scene. There's already enough talk swirling around about your sister. Any scandal you cause to escape this betrothal will impact her."

Geoffrey blew out a harsh breath. Was this why Cranston had asked Holbrook to approach him this evening? Yes, rumors were swirling about Abigail and her daughter, Gemma. His niece had Cranston's eyes. Anyone who met the girl knew immediately that her current husband was her biological father.

There had been much speculation about whether she'd knowingly tried to pass another man's child off as belonging to her deceased husband, the former Viscount Holbrook. Of course, many knew that Baron Cranston had been serving in the army for years and had only recently given up his commission.

Gossip seemed to be split evenly. Men tended to believe Abigail had been willfully dishonest in the whole matter and had deceived her first husband. Women, on the other hand, believed she'd had no choice but to marry someone else when she'd found herself with child after the father had gone off to join the army.

The worst of the speculation was quashed when Cranston's friends had given their unconditional support to the couple after they married. While

Cranston might have been away from England for nearly a decade, he'd somehow acquired quite a few friends in high places. Men most of society didn't want to offend.

So while the rumors had all but abated, that wouldn't remain the case if Geoffrey caused another scandal while attempting to get out of this infernal betrothal.

"Society has never been fair to women. My sister has suffered enough, and I won't do anything to endanger the peace she's found."

He became aware of a hush that had fallen over the ballroom and turned to look at the entrance. He shouldn't have been surprised to find none other than Lydia Pearson standing there, surrounded by her family. Her parents were grinning, basking in the way everyone seemed to be taken with their daughter. Lydia's introduction to society was going just as they'd expected.

He inclined his head toward the entrance. "They're here now."

Holbrook turned to take in the spectacle. Mercifully, he kept his voice low when he spoke. "Your future wife is definitely beautiful. Everyone is staring at her as though no one else exists."

Geoffrey's eyes moved over the crowd, and he

realized the man wasn't exaggerating. Conversation had started again, but gazes were following the family.

He watched as Lord Appleby whispered in his wife's ear before breaking away to join another group of men. When they turned to one of the exits as a group, Geoffrey wanted to groan. So much for escaping to the card room at some point. The last thing he wanted was another lecture from Appleby about how he should be following the man's daughter around like a stray looking for a new owner.

Lady Appleby led her two charges toward a group of women. When he glanced at Holbrook again, he was still watching the women with interest.

"Did Cranston tell you that the betrothal can be broken if both parties are in agreement?"

Holbrook nodded. "He mentioned something to that effect. That's why he's worried you'll try to cause a scandal and force their hand."

Geoffrey frowned. "It's comforting that my brother-in-law considers me such a reprobate and believes I'll act without any consideration about how it will impact my sister."

Holbrook clapped him on the shoulder.

"Cranston is being overprotective. Plus he doesn't really know you."

Geoffrey lifted one brow. "And you do?"

Holbrook grinned. "Not yet, no. But we can remedy that. Become allies."

He examined the viscount. He imagined that as a great nephew to the previous viscount, Holbrook hadn't expected to inherit the title. Still, the man was an easygoing fellow and people seemed to like him. He couldn't imagine he was in desperate need of allies or friends.

Unless… "You have my permission to try to lure Miss Pearson away. She's a beautiful young woman, and I understand your interest."

Holbrook barked out a surprised laugh. "I'm in no hurry to wed, but that was a good attempt on your part. Still, I could be tempted to get to know the older Miss Pearson better."

Geoffrey turned to examine the woman in question. Eleanor Pearson. He'd scarce noticed her during that first meeting when all he'd wanted was to escape that drawing room and all the women's expectant stares. But he was definitely noticing her now, and he realized Holbrook was correct.

It was impossible to miss how much her appearance had improved, and he couldn't help but wonder if she'd purposely dressed in an unflattering manner that morning. She'd been stiff, wearing an awful gown that had made her skin appear sallow. He'd actually thought she was much older than her cousin. Watching her now as she laughed at something Lydia said, he realized she was much closer to his own age.

She was actually very attractive. She didn't possess the delicate beauty of her cousin. No, Eleanor Pearson's beauty was very different but nonetheless undeniable. There was something earthy about her with her dark hair and dark eyes. She was tall, towering over her petite cousin. And her age might allow her a measure of freedom that her younger cousin wouldn't have.

Eleanor Pearson might very well be a woman worth getting to know better. But her intimate acquaintance with his *betrothed*—how he hated that word—meant that Geoffrey would never be able to get to know her intimately. Still, she might become something of an ally. Maybe he could elicit her assistance in convincing Lydia to consider ending the betrothal and marrying someone else.

He circled the room for the next hour, unwilling to fall into the role assigned to him by his father and Appleby. And he certainly wasn't going to be one of the crowd of men, both young and old, who were clamoring for a space on Lydia Pearson's dance card. If she wanted to dance with him, she would save a dance. If not, he wouldn't mourn the loss of the opportunity.

He could feel Lady Appleby's eyes on him as he greeted his brother-in-law's close friends, the Marquess of Lowenbrock and Viscount Ashford. Both men hadn't abandoned their wives as Lord Appleby had done, and it seemed that they, too, were happily married.

That fact had surprised him when Cranston assured him it was possible to marry for love. Geoffrey knew that most marriages made among the ton followed the pattern his father had set for both his betrothal and his sister's first marriage.

He spent some time speaking to several of the acquaintances he'd made during his weeks in London. Some he knew from his time in school, and some he'd met at White's. He avoided the men his father had considered friends, however. He had no desire to be reminded of the man.

During that hour, he watched what was happening with Lydia and Eleanor. Lady Appleby had abandoned the pair soon after their arrival and had spent the time glaring at him and gossiping with a group of older women.

Apparently it was Eleanor's role to act as Lydia's chaperone so the girl's parents could enjoy the evening with others. He filed away that information in case it should prove useful.

Finally, after an hour had passed, he approached the two Miss Pearsons between sets.

Lydia had just joined her cousin after her last partner had left her side with what appeared to be great reluctance. It bothered him that no one had asked Eleanor to partner with them. He'd caught the wistful look in her eyes as she'd watched her young cousin dance. He couldn't say why, but he felt compelled to make up for their oversight.

Eleanor saw him approach and leaned down to whisper in her cousin's ear. Lydia turned to him with a smile and dipped into a curtsy when he reached them.

"It is good to see you, my lord. I was just telling my cousin that I didn't think you were here tonight."

Of course she didn't. She probably imagined he would elbow all other would-be suitors out of the way just to reach her side as soon as she'd been announced.

"Well, here I am."

His smile was aimed at both women. Lydia giggled, but a quick glance at Eleanor told him she wasn't amused. A slight frown had formed between her brows.

"I was speaking with friends, and when I realized you were here, you were caught up with others. I don't suppose you saved a dance for me?"

"Of course. Mama told me to save the supper dance for you."

She offered him her card, and he scribbled his name on the indicated line. He hoped his smile didn't appear false as he murmured something about looking forward to it. Then he turned to Eleanor Pearson.

"And you, Miss Pearson? I hope you have room on your dance card."

Color rose on the woman's cheeks. "I hadn't planned to dance—"

Lydia cut her off. "Oh, you must, Ellie. I hate the idea of your standing here watching me have all the fun. Acting as my chaperone doesn't mean you can't also enjoy yourself tonight."

"Well, perhaps just one dance."

"Excellent," he said before she could change her mind. "I will come collect you when it is time."

He gave them both a polite bow and then turned to leave, pretending to forget that he hadn't signed the woman's card. He was sure there would be a waltz at some point, and he'd return to collect her then. Better to ambush her than to risk Miss Eleanor Pearson finding a way to avoid waltzing with him.

He smiled as he realized he was looking forward to that dance very much.

CHAPTER 5

*E*leanor watched the dancing couples from her position on the edge of the dance floor. The room was a whirlwind of color and movement. The doors to the gardens outside were thrown open, and the air was perfumed with the scent of flowers. Every member of the ton must be there tonight, but the ballroom was large and accommodated the crowd with little difficulty.

She joined a group of women who were also relegated to watching the dancing couples from the side. They'd welcomed her into their midst, their friendly chatter doing much to ease her sense of not belonging. Once upon a time she'd dreamed of being the person who danced every set with a handsome young man. But instead, she was the woman on the edge of spinsterhood.

She was acutely aware of Hargrove's movements. She told herself she was just keeping an eye on the man because he would one day become her cousin through marriage and she was concerned about Lydia's future happiness. But as the evening progressed, she couldn't deny that there was more to her interest.

She chatted with the other women, most of whom were in similar positions. Chaperones to young women who were dancing every set. The dynamic fascinated her. Did all families possess one unmarried female relative whose sole purpose in life was shadowing their young charges?

She couldn't help but be aware of the way Hargrove kept glancing their way. At first she thought he was looking for Lydia, who'd returned to her side between each set. But he did so even when Lydia was dancing. Surely Lord Hargrove should be more interested in watching his betrothed than with what she was doing.

She didn't want to be caught staring at the man, but her attempts at keeping her glances unobtrusive weren't entirely successful. It was as though the man possessed a sixth sense that told him she was looking at him because more often than not, he would turn to meet her gaze. He even had the audacity to wink at her once before turning to chat with a group of men who seemed intent on avoiding dancing altogether. She couldn't understand why they were even at the ball.

But she kept glancing at him, convinced that she'd catch him watching Lydia. Instead, he seemed unconcerned about what his betrothed was doing and with whom. Which left her wondering why he kept looking her way.

She tried to shake off all thought of the earl. Lydia had just left on the arm of another man, and she watched them stroll onto the dance floor. The young lord—really, how could she be expected to remember everyone's name?—was smiling down at her cousin as though he were in possession of the greatest prize in the room. Eleanor didn't normally feel as though twenty-five was a terribly advanced age, but watching the two fresh-faced young people smiling at each other as they took up their positions for what was the first waltz of the evening made her feel ancient.

"Is that boy old enough to be here?"

Eleanor turned to find Hargrove had approached from behind. She covered her mouth with a hand, stifling the laughter that threatened to bubble up at the comment. It was as though he had read her mind.

Why did Hargrove have to be witty as well as handsome?

He held out his arm. "I believe this is our set."

The low timbre of his voice sent a thrill of anticipation through her. One for which she sternly admonished herself. She would enjoy their dance, but she wouldn't start spinning fantasies about this man. Not when he was going to marry Lydia.

"But this is a waltz."

He lifted one brow, and she hated how foolish she sounded.

She lowered her voice and continued. "You should be waltzing with my cousin."

One corner of his mouth lifted in amusement. "Miss Pearson is already dancing with someone else."

He didn't move away, and others were beginning to whisper. She realized she was causing a scene and took his arm. They joined the other couples who were waiting for the music to begin. When they passed a giggling Lydia, whose attention was fixed on her dance partner, she took a deep breath and tried to ignore the nerves that were growing with each passing second.

The opening strains of the music began to play, and she had to force back the desire to flee. Instead, she stepped into Lord Hargrove's arms and sent up a prayer that she wouldn't step on his feet. She'd only waltzed with the dance instructor who'd been hired last year to help Lydia prepare for her debut. The man had been older and very strict about *proper* behavior.

Being in Lord Hargrove's arms, Eleanor felt anything but proper.

For one, she was much taller than other women and had been of an equal height as the dance instructor. But Hargrove made her feel small and delicate. It was a pleasant feeling.

There was a respectable distance between them, but it was impossible to ignore the heat he generated. The hand at her waist felt like it was branding her through her dress. And despite the fact they were both wearing gloves, it was more than a little disconcerting to have her fingers held within his much larger palm.

As he guided her through the dance steps, she couldn't help but notice he was an excellent dance partner. She knew her movements were awkward at first, her worry causing her to hold herself more stiffly than she should. He gave no indication he'd noticed.

He broke the tension that had settled over her by asking, "Are you enjoying the evening, Miss Pearson?"

"I'm enjoying it more now that I'm actually dancing." And she was, even if she felt as though the two of them shouldn't be waltzing.

His eyes crinkled at the corners as he smiled at her. "I am happy to be of service."

They made one turn about the ballroom in silence before he spoke again. "I believe it is now your turn to continue the conversation."

Her mind was blank, so she relied on one of the staples of pleasant discourse. "It is unseasonably warm for this time of year. Do you not think so?"

He chuckled. "So tell me, Miss Pearson, just how close are you to your cousin?"

His question had the effect of both calming and unsettling her nerves. Lydia was a common subject of conversation among the men of her acquaintance—the women too if she were being truthful. It was a familiar refrain. But she couldn't deny she was disappointed that he'd only asked her to dance because he wanted to discuss Lydia.

"We are very close."

He executed a quick turn. It was so expertly done she hadn't had time to wonder if she was going to trip until they'd returned to the standard steps of the dance. But she did notice that she was now a fraction closer to him. There was still a respectable distance between them, but she couldn't deny her proximity to him unsettled her.

"What are your cousin's feelings about our betrothal? You can be honest with me."

He looked so calm, and it annoyed her that he was totally unaffected when she could barely breathe. "She thinks you're old."

He let out a bark of laughter. "She'll have her pick of suitors this season."

His lack of concern bothered her. "Does she need suitors when she already has you?"

His eyes narrowed as he examined her. "Your uncle has told me that she doesn't wish anyone to learn about the agreement."

Eleanor sighed. "If you're concerned that she won't do her duty—"

"Actually, the opposite is true."

Eleanor had no idea what he was saying. The man was speaking in riddles. "You're worried she'll do her duty?"

"I don't wish to wed."

His gaze was steady on hers, and she could tell he was speaking the truth. Her mouth dropped open, but then she snapped it closed.

"You don't wish to wed at all?"

He shrugged as he swept them past a dancing pair who almost stumbled into them. "I suppose I'll marry one day. It was quite a shock to learn it would be quite so soon."

She could only stare at him. "I don't understand. Surely your father would have told you about the betrothal."

His lips twisted to the side in a wry grimace. "I see you are unaware of what happens in far too many families. Your uncle's behavior is very unusual. He's taking his daughter's preferences in mind and allowing her a measure of freedom this season merely because she wishes it. My father, on the other hand, saw no need to consult me when he made this arrangement."

Surely she wasn't hearing him correctly. "It's my understanding that it's been in place for several years."

"And I learned about it on his deathbed."

She felt a flash of sympathy for the man. She knew that women were often given away in marriage agreements that would see them doomed to an unhappy life. But she'd never imagined that the same could be true for men.

She could understand now why he didn't seem affected by Lydia's beauty. He didn't wish to wed. It wouldn't matter who the woman was when he was being forced into the arrangement. And to learn of it just before coming into his title, when he no doubt expected to enjoy years of freedom, must have been a bitter blow.

Still, if he was going to be forced to wed, at least his father had made an excellent match. "I can assure you that you will be very happy with my cousin."

His eyes roamed over her face. "Perhaps. But it is entirely possible that she might find someone more to her liking this season."

She smiled sympathetically, understanding his fears, and sought to reassure him. "I can be an ally for you. I will let Lydia know that you have behaved quite pleasantly with me. And that my impressions of you are positive. I can urge her to give you serious consideration. Even if you are quite old."

She'd hoped to elicit a laugh from him. Instead, his mouth curved to the side as though she'd said something wrong.

"Please don't."

She didn't know what to say to that. The silence stretched between them, and as time passed, she grew more uncomfortable. But she couldn't think of anything to say that would ease the tension.

It didn't help that Hargrove was staring down at her as though he was trying to read her mind. Finally the music swelled and he executed a complicated turn. If he'd been a less competent partner, she would have found herself spinning into another couple. Instead, he pulled her back into his arms.

She let out a small huff of laughter. "When our dance instructor tried to show me how to do that, I ended up spinning into the wall."

"He must not have been very good. You're doing very well now."

He was being generous, but it wouldn't be polite to enter into an argument on the subject. "I have an excellent partner."

He pulled her an inch closer, and her breath hitched in her throat. "I won't let you stumble, Miss Pearson."

Something about the low timbre of his voice, the way his eyes narrowed on her lips when she licked them, had her heart doing an odd little flip.

Which was a disastrous reaction to have to the man her cousin was going to marry.

"My cousin loves to dance," she blurted out. "I hope the supper dance is also a waltz so the two of you can begin to get to know one another better."

He didn't reply, but he did increase the space between them. A small, selfish part of her soul was displeased at the growing distance—both physical and emotional—that had come about as a result of her words. But they both needed a reminder that even though he might not wish it, he *was* going to marry Lydia.

CHAPTER 6

Geoffrey strolled into White's around noon. He wouldn't have bothered, but Holbrook had let him know he'd be there this morning. And Geoffrey needed someone with whom to discuss his current dilemma. Someone who wasn't Abigail. He couldn't burden her with this anymore when there wasn't anything she could do about the matter. She'd already suffered under Father's dictates. It was up to him to get himself through this.

He spotted Holbrook chatting with a group of men who were ensconced by the club's famous bow window. Before Geoffrey could join them, Holbrook spotted him. He said something to the group and came to join him.

They met by the fireplace and settled into armchairs.

Holbrook leaned back in his chair and examined him. "I see you finally rolled out of bed."

He shrugged, refusing to apologize. They both knew that most of the ton were still abed. "It was a late night. How about you? I didn't see you leave."

Holbrook grinned. "I disappeared into the card room. Your future father-in-law was there all night. He's a shrewd card player, never wagering more than he could afford to lose. And he won more often than not."

That wasn't what he wanted to hear. Things would be much easier if Appleby were more prone to acting before he thought things through.

"When was this? The last time I saw you, you seemed to be content dancing." One of those women with whom he'd danced had been Eleanor. He couldn't say why that had bothered him. It wasn't as though he had any say when it came to her dance partners.

"I tired of it long before the supper dance. It became quite tedious trying to avoid all the young women debuting this year who are desperate to wed. There's far more fun to be had with the older women who are more open to other arrangements. But enough about me. How did things go with you?"

He shrugged. "I stayed until the end."

Holbrook frowned. "Good God, man, don't make me pull it out of you. What happened? You were still skulking about the edges of the room when I quit the field."

He tsked. "Abigail didn't tell me you were such a gossip."

One corner of Holbrook's mouth rose. "It's not gossip if I'm asking the person directly for information. Now spill the details."

Geoffrey shook his head. "There isn't much to tell. I spoke to people and I danced a few times."

"They're already calling Miss Lydia Pearson the diamond of the season. Did you dance with her more than once?"

Geoffrey let out a frustrated breath. "By the time I made it round to her, I was hoping all her dances had already been spoken for. But she saved the supper dance for me."

"She was that sure of you then?"

"She honestly didn't see me until I approached. She was so busy with her other admirers. I was amazed to find her and her cousin alone for a brief moment."

"But she saved the supper dance for you. That's an announcement to others that you hold a preferential place in her esteem."

His lips twisted to the side. "If I'd waited twenty more minutes, she would have given someone else that honor. She only waited that long because her mother had instructed her to leave that dance open for me."

A footman approached then, and their conversation halted as they both asked for coffee. More people were arriving at the club, so he wasn't sure how much longer they'd be able to continue this conversation. He didn't want anyone overhearing them. Appleby had said that Lydia didn't want people to know about their betrothal until the end of the season. That gave Geoffrey a few months to find a way out of it.

They waited as the footman poured their drinks and then moved off to the group still sitting by the bow window, the members of which were becoming increasingly boisterous. From the snippets he could overhear, it had to do with one of the bills that had been introduced to the House of Lords. He should be paying more attention to such matters, but his upcoming marriage was consuming all his thoughts.

Holbrook drank from his cup before continuing with his quest to uncover every detail about the evening. "Was she glad to see you?"

He shrugged. "From what I could tell, she showed me no preference."

"And how does that make you feel? Any second thoughts about ending the betrothal?"

"I feel deuced relieved. It means there's an excellent chance someone else can lure her away from me. And as you saw, many are willing to try."

Holbrook shook his head. "Do you know why Appleby is so set on this match? No offense, and heaven knows you outrank me as an earl, but Miss Pearson would have no difficulty securing a marquess or a duke."

"I've wondered the same thing, so I paid my solicitor another visit."

"And?"

Geoffrey leaned forward, his elbows on his knees. "I believe it has to do with land. It isn't outright specified in the betrothal agreement, but I learned that several years ago, Appleby sold off most of his unentailed land to my father."

"That would be it then. It sounds like Appleby wanted to secure as much as he could for future generations. Since he doesn't have a male heir, everything will go to someone else."

He nodded. "That's what I figure as well. He sold off the property that wasn't tied up to my father with the understanding that his daughter will marry me. He could therefore keep as much as he could for his direct descendants."

Holbrook frowned. "And your solicitor didn't tell you this back when he told you about the betrothal agreement?"

Geoffrey resisted the urge to bark out a bitter laugh. "No. It appears the man is still loyal to carrying out my father's wishes."

"You need a new solicitor. I can give you the name of mine."

He nodded. "I'll be looking into that soon. I don't need another person in my life trying to control what I do."

The Earl of Stanley sauntered into the room then, and Geoffrey's eyes narrowed on the man. He'd been at the Clarington ball yesterday and the germ of an idea began to form.

"Stanley," he called out when it looked like he was about to join the group by the window.

The man turned toward him and nodded a greeting before joining them.

Geoffrey introduced him to Holbrook and then examined him as the earl dropped into an armchair. They were the same age and had been classmates at Cambridge. He was a nice enough fellow, but he had a competitive streak that could make him a little hard to take at times.

His father was a marquess, however, and Geoffrey had heard that the man exerted a great deal of pressure on his son to ensure he was the best at everything. For some reason, Stanley thrived under that pressure.

Holbrook smiled at the man. "So how long have you known Hargrove here? Do you have any embarrassing stories to share about him?"

Geoffrey scowled but Stanley laughed. "More than a few since we were classmates, but I daresay he could say the same about me. I think I'll save my storytelling for a time when he can't embarrass me as well."

Holbrook frowned. "That's too bad. I'll have to seek you out another time then."

Stanley leaned back in his chair and examined the two of them. "What are you fellows up to today? I think I saw you both at Clarington's ball last night."

Geoffrey nodded. "We were there. We were just talking about how it might be time to seek out brides."

Holbrook's eyes widened a fraction at the falsehood, but he didn't deny the statement. Good man.

Stanley examined him, and Geoffrey could see exactly what he was thinking. "Who did you have in mind?"

He lifted one shoulder in a casual shrug. He hoped his meager acting abilities would be enough to carry this charade. "My father was good friends with Appleby. I think he always hoped for a match between me and the man's daughter."

Most of his classmates were aware that he wasn't fond of his father, so he added, "I've never been one to fall in line with his plans, but after meeting the young woman, I think I can make an exception in this case."

Stanley was almost unnaturally still. Finally he said, "I danced with Miss Pearson myself last night."

"Did you?" In truth, Geoffrey hadn't bothered to keep track of all the men who'd danced with Lydia. He hadn't really cared. But now he did.

"Yes. In fact, I'm going to be calling on her later today."

Holbrook chuckled. "You and every other eligible bachelor in town."

Geoffrey watched the man carefully as he said, "I was going to call on her myself."

He didn't want to, but Appleby would expect it, especially after he'd danced with his daughter yesterday. Still, if he could stoke this man's competitive streak, the visit would be worth it.

Stanley stiffened. His eyes had narrowed, and Geoffrey had to force himself not to grin. The earl didn't like to lose. He would marry Lydia to best a rival. It helped that Miss Pearson was already being called the diamond of the season.

Stanley stood, clearly wanting to get going on his new mission in life—besting Geoffrey at winning the lovely Lydia Pearson's hand.

"I'd planned to meet some friends in the billiard room and I'm running late. But I'll be seeing you at the Appleby town house later."

Stanley took his leave with a small bow. Geoffrey could no longer hide his grin as he watched the man stride away as though the room were on fire.

Holbrook waited until Stanley had exited the

morning room before speaking. "You are an evil genius."

Geoffrey laughed. "It was too easy. The man hates to lose. And when the prize is someone as sought after as Miss Pearson…" He shrugged. "Thank goodness Stanley hasn't changed. He was always such a nuisance."

"And you have no qualms about siccing him on Miss Pearson?"

Geoffrey shrugged again. "Aside from his drive to always come out on top, he's a nice enough fellow. I've never heard anyone speak ill of him. He'll make Lydia the perfect husband."

"And he'll be a marquess one day. Do they have money?"

He nodded. "An obscene amount of it. Appleby would be a fool to turn him down just so he could insist on moving forward with a match between his daughter and me."

"And the land he sold to your father?"

"The solicitor is dragging his feet on providing me with the details, but I'm sure it can't be worth more than what his daughter would stand to gain marrying Stanley."

Holbrook shook his head. "Life doesn't always

go according to plan. They could find that they don't suit."

He tried not to wince at the thought. "Then I'll have to find someone else. It won't be difficult. I'm sure their Grosvenor Square town house will be filled with men this afternoon, all vying for the role of future husband to Miss Pearson."

CHAPTER 7

Lord Hargrove called promptly at four thirty p.m. He'd been one of the many suitors who had called on Lydia the previous afternoon and was given permission to take Lydia for a ride at Hyde Park today during the fashionable hour.

Aunt Helen's dictate that they needed to keep him waiting this afternoon made no sense. Worse, Eleanor feared it would cause him to reconsider the apparent change of heart he'd had.

After their conversation at the Clarington ball, she'd been surprised to hear him issue the invitation. He'd confessed that he didn't want to marry Lydia, but he must have changed his mind. At the very least it seemed that he'd decided it best to get to know her better.

The supper dance at the ball had been another waltz. Eleanor had stood off to the side and watched the two of them dance. They were opposite in every way, but no one could deny that they made a lovely couple. Hargrove was tall and dark-haired while Lydia was petite and fair-haired. They complemented each other perfectly.

Now she and Lydia waited in the music room. Lydia was wearing a white day dress while Eleanor had reverted back to her customary attire of a simple morning gown. But at least it wasn't the horrid yellow one. Lydia had made good on her word and had given it to one of the maids. This one was a simple dress of blue muslin, but the color was flattering against her skin.

When the footman informed them that Lord Hargrove had arrived, they waited ten minutes, just as Aunt Helen had ordered. Eleanor hated the idea of keeping him waiting, and the minutes stretched interminably.

Finally they were allowed to leave the music room. Aunt Helen and Lydia walked arm in arm to join their guest in the drawing room, and Eleanor followed.

She had to bite her tongue to keep from apologizing for keeping him waiting. Instead, she took up her position next to Lydia and did her best to disappear. Normally she didn't have to try, but Hargrove had a bad habit of actually looking at her and including her in their conversation as they chatted about the weather and various balls they would be attending.

Finally Aunt Helen released them with effusive smiles at Hargrove. He bowed politely and then offered Lydia his arm. Eleanor tried to ignore the small twinge of emotion as she walked behind them out to his carriage. She absolutely was not jealous.

Hargrove helped Lydia up into the open-air carriage before turning to her and holding out his hand. Eleanor hesitated a moment, her thoughts going back to how it had felt to place her hand in his when they'd waltzed. Pushing back the memory, she accepted his offered hand.

This man shouldn't make her so nervous. Despite the reservations he'd confessed to her, he would be marrying her cousin at the end of the season. When that happened, she'd be seeing the two of them together often.

His thumb moved over the back of her hand as she lifted her foot onto the first step, and the shock of the caress caused her to stumble. His fingers tightened on hers, and their eyes met and held for several long moments.

"Did you hurt yourself, Ellie?" Lydia's genuine concern broke the tension between them.

Heat rose into Eleanor's cheeks as she climbed into the carriage. "I misjudged the height of the step, but I am well."

Lydia smiled. "I did that last year and turned my ankle."

Hargrove sprang up into the carriage and settled onto the bench seat across from them.

Lydia kept up a constant stream of chatter as the carriage progressed to the park. The rumble of Hargrove's voice as he added a word here and there had her struggling not to squirm in her seat despite the fact that his words were a little distant, though polite. Lydia didn't seem to notice, but Eleanor couldn't help remembering the way he'd pulled her close when they were dancing and vowed not to let her stumble. He'd caught her again just now, but he'd also been the cause of her misstep. She was certain it was an accident, however. A product of her overactive imagination.

Eleanor kept her eyes cast down during the ride,

resisting the almost overwhelming temptation to stare at Hargrove. She had to keep reminding herself that she was only there because she was acting as Lydia's chaperone. Hargrove would never call on Eleanor and escort her to Hyde Park.

Grosvenor Square was right next to the park, and so they soon reached their destination.

Lydia's eyes scanned the crowds. "I've never been here during the fashionable hour. I didn't expect there to be so many carriages. Oh, and you can also stroll! Can we walk?"

Eleanor smiled. It was impossible not to become caught up in her cousin's enthusiasm. She also knew that Lydia loved chatting with people and she would hate being cut off from everyone if they remained in the carriage.

"Of course," he said before turning to instruct the driver to meet them at the end of the promenade.

He helped them down, and Eleanor was careful not to trip. Of course, this time she didn't allow herself to overreact at the feeling of her hand in his. He certainly had not caressed her hand with his thumb. She'd imagined the sensation.

He offered Lydia his arm, but his eyes met

Eleanor's over her cousin's head. Eleanor forced herself to look away and wait for the couple to pass her. As their chaperone, she would follow behind them. Invisible.

CHAPTER 8

Geoffrey found his gaze continually drawn to the older Miss Pearson. He'd waltzed with both Lydia and her cousin during the Clarington ball, and he'd enjoyed dancing with Eleanor more. She intrigued him but he couldn't say why. It was clear she was completely devoted to her cousin, and yet he still found himself thinking that he could bring her around to his way of thinking.

It was impossible to ignore her despite the fact she seemed to go out of her way to fade into the background, as she was doing now. For some reason, that fact annoyed him. He attributed it to the way she seemed to believe that she was too old to be noticed by members of the opposite sex. Yet his sister was older than her and was newly wed and with child. It bothered him to think that many would have placed Abigail in the same category as Eleanor—women who were too old to consider for anything other than a quick tumble.

Lydia Pearson was clearly the beauty of the family, but no one would say that Eleanor was unattractive. Her medium brown hair made her pale skin appear almost translucent. And when he'd stared into her brown eyes while dancing with her, he couldn't help but feel that they hid all manner of secrets.

With the younger Miss Pearson, he felt as though he already knew everything there was to know about her. She was pleasant enough, but he found it impossible to care much about the things that engrossed her. Right now she was gazing about, concerned only with learning who else was there.

But Eleanor… He almost felt compelled to expose her secrets. She kept everything carefully hidden, and he wanted to know what she was thinking. He was very aware of her just on the other side of Lydia, one step behind them. The circumspect chaperone.

He glanced at Lydia, who was waving at

everyone she passed. But there was a fervent, searching quality to her gaze that had him wondering if she was looking for someone in particular.

"Do you read, Miss Pearson?" he asked.

Lydia scrunched her nose. "No. Ellie is always trying to encourage me to read more, but I've never been a great reader. And don't even get me started on poetry."

She gave a small shudder that he supposed was cute. But it made him feel sad for her. He couldn't understand why society tried to discourage reading in young women. It was a pastime he enjoyed as well.

"So how do you pass the time?"

"I like to practice on the pianoforte. And I enjoy drawing, but I am not nearly as talented as Eleanor."

He waited for her to pick up the thread of conversation, but she said nothing else. She was more interested in waving and smiling at the people they passed than trying to get to know him. He had the sudden image of being bound forever to a woman who barely spoke to him. That wouldn't do.

"Your father told me about your plans for this season."

He had her attention now. "My plans?"

"He told me you were intent on enjoying the coming months to the fullest and that you didn't wish to make our *arrangement* known."

Her mouth turned into a pout that he was sure would have many stumbling over themselves to ease her worries. "I hope you don't mind. But I thought it most unfair to expect us to wed so soon. My first season is only starting."

He nodded. "I understand completely. And I agree with you."

She frowned. "You do?"

"Of course. One can hardly expect you'd be content to shackle yourself to someone you've only just met. It is perfectly reasonable for you to want some time to enjoy yourself."

She was nodding now. "I'm so glad you agree. Mama said you might want to press the matter of our marriage."

He wished she'd stop speaking in such an animated fashion. People were already looking their way. Before long, everyone would know they were betrothed.

"I would never want to force you into something you don't wish to do. You'll only have one first season. It is only right that you should enjoy it."

He hesitated a moment, wondering how much to press the issue. He didn't want to offend Miss Pearson and risk the wrath of her parents. He needed her on his side.

"It is clear that your mother dotes on you. And when I spoke to your father, I could see that he cares for you very much."

Lydia smiled. "I am most fortunate. Mama and Papa are wonderful. And of course I also have Ellie. She's so patient with me." She lowered her voice. "I'm sure I try her patience at times, but she never shows it."

He tucked away that little nugget of information about Eleanor. "Your parents would do anything for you?"

Lydia nodded, content in her knowledge that Lord and Lady Appleby would move heaven and earth for her. But would they agree to break their agreement if that was Miss Pearson's wish?

"I am not one to force someone to marry me if they don't wish to. The notion of forced betrothals is abhorrent to me."

Lydia's attention had wandered off to a couple who were engaged in what appeared to be a heated disagreement, but his words had her looking up at him again. Her brows drew together. "Are you saying that you find the idea of marrying me abhorrent?"

He cursed silently. He would have to be more careful with his choice of words. "I'm saying that neither one of us knows the other. It is quite possible that you'll find you don't wish to marry when the season ends."

She weighed his words for a minute, and he forced himself to wait. When she finally spoke, her eyes were clouded. "But we are already betrothed."

He'd already gone this far and had to continue. They might not have another opportunity to speak on this subject. He cast a quick glance at Eleanor, whose brows were furrowed together in concentration. He and Lydia had both softened their voices, and he hoped she couldn't overhear their conversation. He suspected she would drag Lydia from his side if she thought he was speaking to her cousin about the possibility of ending their betrothal.

"My solicitor has looked over the contract. The betrothal can be broken if both sides are in agreement."

Lydia's eyes widened. "So you're saying…"

"That no decisions need to be made right now despite what your parents might believe. You should take these next few months to look around. You were planning to enjoy your season anyway, so nothing will change there. But if you find someone else who captures your interest…" He raised one shoulder in a casual shrug. "If you fall in love with another, I will understand and bow out."

She glanced sideways at him, and it was clear she didn't know whether to believe him. "I thought men didn't believe in such nonsense. That they married only for practical reasons."

He couldn't hold back a small smile. "I used to think it a foolish notion to marry for love. But I've seen my sister and her husband prove that assumption incorrect. There is no question in my mind that they are in love with each other. Theirs is a happy marriage."

Lydia smiled up at him, a look of wonder on her face. It seemed to say that she was seeing him for the first time. "And you want that for yourself."

"And for you as well. There's no reason to tie ourselves to a practical union formed by our parents before we'd met when we could both have more."

"And what if I decide that I *want* to marry you?"

Geoffrey stared down at the woman holding on to his arm. It wouldn't be a hardship to marry her. They could probably be content enough together. But he hadn't lied when he'd spoken about wanting what his sister had found with Baron Cranston. What the pair had found in one another. Geoffrey might tease them about their behavior whenever he visited them, but watching the way they looked at one another... He didn't think he would ever have that with Lydia Pearson.

He felt the space between his shoulders itch and had the uncanny feeling that he could feel Eleanor's eyes on him. He forced himself not to turn and look at her and kept his gaze on Lydia. "We have time before you decide. Months. Let's not be hasty, not when your future happiness is at stake."

Lydia considered his words for some time before letting out a sigh. "What you say makes a great deal of sense."

He forced back a grin. "So?"

She nodded. "We can have this discussion again at the end of the season. And I'm relieved that I have your permission to consider other suitors."

He raised one brow. "You were already entertaining a large number of them yesterday when I called."

She laughed. "I wasn't actually entertaining the thought that I might be free to wed someone else. But now everything is different. Of course, I'll have to speak to Ellie about this."

A zing went through Geoffrey, and he told himself it was just alarm. Eleanor could very well try to dissuade her cousin from looking elsewhere. She'd already told him that she would try to help convince Lydia about what a wonderful match they would make.

"Will she tell your parents? They could very well insist we marry straight away if they knew we were discussing this."

Lydia smiled at him as though he were daft. "Oh no, Ellie is a dear. She wouldn't do anything to hurt me."

CHAPTER 9

An odd sense of disquiet settled over Eleanor for the rest of the day, and she couldn't quite say why. First it had bothered her to watch Lydia promenade through Hyde Park on Lord Hargrove's arm. She told herself it wasn't because *she* wanted to be on his arm. She would never want to promote her own happiness over that of her cousin's.

No, it was simply that witnessing the two as they spoke in low tones to one another, ignoring everyone around them for long stretches of time as they entered into their own world, had made her realize that she wanted to experience that as well.

But not with Lord Hargrove, of course.

And then after they'd returned home, Lydia had

shared with her the topic of that intense conversation. Eleanor didn't know quite what she'd expected. Hargrove had told her that he didn't wish to marry Lydia, but she'd begun to think he was just being stubborn. It would have been a shock to learn about the betrothal after his father had kept it a secret for so many years. But Lydia was lovely and delightful. Eleanor was sure that all he would need was to spend some time with her cousin and he, too, would fall under her spell.

She'd thought she was witnessing his change of heart yesterday at Hyde Park. Instead, he'd told Lydia that she was free to entertain other suitors and that he would agree to end the betrothal if that was her desire.

She hadn't expected him to share that information with Lydia. And instead of being upset at the idea that the very handsome, very eligible Hargrove wouldn't be one of the men eagerly pursuing her that season, Lydia had been delighted.

The entire situation baffled Eleanor. She would have been heartbroken if she were in her cousin's place.

They attended a musicale that evening, and Lydia had delighted the assembled guests with her skill on the pianoforte. Eleanor had never been musically inclined, something for which she was infinitely grateful because it meant she would never be called to perform in front of others. Lydia, however, thrived under the attention.

Lord Hargrove had already told them he wouldn't be in attendance at the small gathering that evening, so Eleanor had been saved the worry about seeing him again. But in the end it didn't really matter because she couldn't stop thinking about the man.

After returning home for the night, she fell into bed with one goal in mind. To fall asleep and leave thoughts of Lord Hargrove and his perplexing behavior behind her.

She woke bright and early the next morning, long before the other members of the household. Her quiet mornings suited her just fine. She enjoyed her private pursuits when her aunt and cousin weren't making demands on her time. And later she would be visiting Hatchards circulating library where she'd take advantage of the subscription she'd purchased with some of her pin money.

She asked for breakfast to be sent up to her room and then turned her attention to working on her latest drawing. Mornings were the only opportunity she'd had to sketch since coming to London.

Of late she'd been working on perfecting her skills at drawing people.

She had several drawings of her aunt and uncle, and of course Lydia was a favorite model. She'd even tried her hand at drawing herself. But today she had another model in mind. Lord Hargrove.

She hesitated only a moment before giving in to the temptation. She sketched quickly from memory, her pencil moving over the page with smooth strokes as she tried to capture the man. She told herself she could give it to Lydia as a gift if the two did decide to proceed with their betrothal. And if she didn't, he wouldn't be the first man she'd drawn. She often drew pictures of neighbors and family friends, both male and female.

She'd intended it to be a quick sketch with just enough details to make it clear who the subject was. It wasn't until she found herself trying to capture the glint she'd seen in his eyes when they were waltzing that she realized this drawing was more detailed than she'd planned.

She frowned at the image, considering whether she should stop. But no, she was gripped with the need to finish it.

An hour passed before she stared down at the image with a critical eye. She'd drawn him as he'd appeared yesterday, sitting on the bench seat of the carriage opposite her and Lydia. But in the drawing he wasn't smiling at her cousin, that infernal twinkle in his eyes, but at her.

With a sigh, she put down her pencil. She couldn't just sit here all day, staring at the man's image. She took care to place it in the middle of the small stack of her other drawings.

Voices in the hallway told her that the rest of the household was now up. She glanced at the mantel clock and saw it was almost noon. She'd have to hurry before it was too late for her to carry out her other errand for the day.

She had her aunt's permission to visit Hatchards bookshop. Several men had indicated their desire to call on Lydia this afternoon, and Aunt Helen would be overseeing those visits. Eleanor's attendance wasn't required.

She made her way to Lydia's room to see how her cousin was faring. But she needn't have worried. Many of the new dresses they'd ordered had arrived, and Lydia's maid was already pinning up her hair. Her cousin was in her element, chatting about whom she hoped would call later that afternoon. She didn't even mention Lord Hargrove.

After listening to her cousin's musings for

several minutes, Eleanor said her goodbyes. One of the maids, a young woman who was new to the staff, would be accompanying her to Hatchards, which was only a twenty-minute walk from Grosvenor Square.

At first Eleanor tried to engage the young woman in conversation. But when the maid looked horrified at the idea of having to converse with her, Eleanor made a comment about the weather and then let the matter drop. She didn't miss the way the young woman's shoulders seemed to sag with relief.

Eleanor turned to the maid when they reached the bookshop. "Will you be coming in with me?"

The maid shook her head. "Cook has a few items she wants me to buy, but if you need me, I can make those purchases later."

Eleanor waved off her concern. "It's a book-shop. I'm sure I'll be fine."

They made arrangements to meet outside the store in one hour's time, and then Eleanor stepped through the front doors. She took a moment to close her eyes and inhale deeply. There was some-thing special about being in a bookstore that had all her senses tingling with excitement.

She smiled at another woman who gave her a

little wave before turning back to the book she was leafing through. Eleanor had seen her the last time she was here, when she'd been allowed exactly five minutes to dash inside and purchase her subscription. There hadn't been time to do more than that because they were newly arrived in London and on their way to Bond Street to visit the modiste.

But today there were no restrictions placed on her time. As long as she was home early enough to prepare for the evening's entertainment—she couldn't remember whether they'd be seeing a play tonight or going to a rout—her absence from home wouldn't be missed.

She moved farther into the store, almost at a loss as to where she should begin. It seemed unfair that she could only borrow two books. How would she ever choose?

The murmur of voices from the reading room tucked into the back of the shop indicated that a group was having a discussion about a book they'd all read. She felt a wistful pang. Perhaps one day she could join in on one of those discussions. But today she wasn't brave enough to wander into the room to see which book held their interest.

She turned and made her way to the section of the store that held the newest editions. A number of books were displayed on a table. She began on one side, determined to look through each one before making her choices. Half an hour passed in this fashion. At the end of that time, she found herself staring down at the five books in her hand, trying to decide which ones to put back.

A masculine voice sounded close behind her. "Miss Pearson."

She hadn't expected to see anyone she knew here. She turned and came face-to-face with Lord Hargrove. Something about the way his blue eyes moved down her body before returning to her face unsettled her.

"What are you doing here?"

He raised one brow, and she chastised herself for her abrupt tone.

"Excuse me, but I was surprised to see you here. I expected that you'd be calling on Lydia this afternoon."

His head tilted to one side as he examined her. She wished he would stop staring at her with that unsettling gaze.

"I'm sure your cousin won't be lacking for visitors today. I doubt she'll miss me."

His words made no sense to her. It didn't seem possible that Lydia wouldn't miss him. He was very handsome, eligible, and the man she was going to marry despite what he'd told her yesterday in Hyde Park.

Eleanor wouldn't say as much to him though. She needed to change the subject. She was in no mood to hear yet another lecture about how he didn't wish to wed.

She released an exaggerated sigh. "I wish I could borrow all these books."

"Why don't you?"

"Because my subscription only allows me to borrow two books at a time. I shall have to place three back and hope they're still available when I return next week."

He held his hand out, clearly wanting to see what she'd chosen. She winced inwardly as she did so. "Don't judge me too harshly."

She'd selected one book of poetry and four novels. She already knew she couldn't put back the book of poetry. If her aunt asked to see what she'd borrowed, that was the book she'd show her. It wasn't that Eleanor didn't like poetry, but Uncle already had several volumes in the library she could read. But he had none of the novels she'd come to love. The so-called "horrid" novels. She knew her aunt wouldn't approve of them.

"These are all quite good," he said. "I see your dilemma."

He'd surprised her. "You read novels?"

He shrugged. "They're entertaining. Why wouldn't I read them?"

"Which was your favorite?"

He looked through the four and handed her Ann Radcliffe's *Mysteries of Udolpho*. "Are you set on the poetry?"

She let out another sigh. "I'm afraid so. Aunt Helen will want to see what I've burrowed. She doesn't approve of *novels*." She said the word the way her aunt would, and he chuckled at her scandalous tone.

"You seem to have a good head on your shoulders. I don't think you'll start imagining that your uncle's town house is haunted."

They chatted for a few more minutes about the books. Finally she put back three, keeping the book of poetry and the novel he'd recommended. He wandered off, heading toward the counter. She wanted to follow, curious about what he was saying to the store clerk.

After a few minutes, he turned to face her. He dipped his head and then strode from the store. The entire encounter had left her feeling a little disconcerted. He hadn't taken any books with him. Had he told the clerk to have them sent to his house?

She made her way to the counter with her two books. It was best she leave now or she'd find herself in another conundrum, her arms filled with books and still able to borrow only two of them.

She placed the books on the counter so the clerk could record her choices.

He frowned. "Only these two books?"

Eleanor nodded.

The clerk was a middle-aged man, slightly round of stature, but he seemed kindly. The man cleared his throat before saying, "Your subscription has been upgraded. You can borrow five books today."

She frowned in confusion. Her aunt or uncle wouldn't have done this. "I don't understand…"

"The man who was just here, the one you were speaking to. He said he was a friend of the family. He arranged for the extra books."

Lord Hargrove. He'd done this for her. She felt a strange mixture of emotions upon discovering his generosity. Heady excitement, worry that perhaps she shouldn't accept this. But she would, of course. He was, after all, a friend of the family. And friends gave each other small gifts all the time.

She shouldn't read anything into his act of kindness.

"His father was friends with my uncle."

The clerk nodded. "I see. If you're sure you only want these two books…"

She shook her head. She wouldn't turn down Lord Hargrove's generous gift. "I know exactly which books I want."

She turned back to the table to collect the other three books, wondering when she would see Hargrove again. She would have to find some way to thank him.

CHAPTER 10

The next week passed in a whirl of events. Balls, routs, morning calls. Eleanor enjoyed the occasional outing, but the season had only just started and she was already looking forward to it being over.

Lydia, of course, was popular and much sought after. One man in particular seemed intent on winning her hand, and it wasn't the man to whom she was betrothed. The Earl of Stanley had been at every event they'd attended and went out of his way to single out Lydia.

The same couldn't be said for Lord Hargrove, whom Eleanor had only seen at two events, both of them balls. He'd asked her to dance both times, but neither occasion had been a waltz and she hadn't been able to say more than a few words to him, let alone thank him for his generosity at Hatchards.

He'd waltzed with Eleanor that first evening because he'd wanted to broach the subject of ending his betrothal to her cousin. After speaking to Lydia herself on the matter during their outing in Hyde Park, he wouldn't need to speak to Eleanor about it again. Still, it was nice to be asked to dance.

But today Eleanor would be visiting Hatchards again. She'd made it through all the books she'd borrowed—she had to occupy her time somehow while Lydia was entertaining suitors.

She'd been filled with expectation all morning. She told herself it was because the bookshop was a center of calm during the whirlwind of the social season. But when she walked into the store, her gaze swept over all the customers currently browsing.

She could no longer deny that she'd been hoping to see Lord Hargrove again. The likelihood of running into him a second time was slim, of course, but that didn't stop her from ensuring her visit was planned for the same time as last week's.

He'd mentioned that he liked to frequent the shop, and a small part of her mind had filed away that information. Short of making arrangements with the man to meet her, it was the best she could do.

She stopped first at the main desk to return the books she'd borrowed last week. That task completed, she headed toward the reading room at the back of the shop. She hadn't ventured that far last week and wanted to explore. And if Lord Hargrove was there, she'd finally have the chance to thank him.

Her first impression of the room was that it was larger than she'd expected. Like the front room, the reading room was filled with floor-to-ceiling bookshelves. But interspersed throughout the room were several seating arrangements.

Tucked away in one corner was a group of women who were chatting about one of the books she'd just finished reading. Eleanor was tempted to join them, but then she spotted Lord Hargrove. He was standing before one of the bookshelves and seemed to be scanning the titles.

A smile spread across her face and she took a step in his direction. She froze in place, however, when he leaned down to speak to the woman who was standing next to him. The woman laughed, amused with what he'd said, and linked her arm through his.

Eleanor's stomach hollowed at the sight, and she couldn't help but feel foolish. It seemed that Lord Hargrove made it a habit to charm women in bookshops. Eleanor wasn't special at all.

She needed to turn around and leave now before he saw her. Instead, she found herself rooted in place, unable to look away from the two people before her. Was this woman the reason Hargrove didn't want to marry Lydia?

The pair turned, and Eleanor's eyes immediately settled on the woman's rounded belly. Her gaze took in her appearance, and she realized this must be Lord Hargrove's sister. The woman's eyes were the precise same shade of blue.

When she looked at Hargrove again, he was smiling at her as though he'd read her thoughts and was amused.

"Miss Pearson, it is good to see you today," he said when she approached. "Allow me to introduce you to my sister, Baroness Cranston. Abigail, this is Miss Eleanor Pearson."

The baroness's curiosity was evident as they

exchanged greetings. "I thought that perhaps you were the other Miss Pearson."

Eleanor couldn't tell whether Hargrove had told his sister about the betrothal. If he had, surely she wouldn't have confused Eleanor for Lydia.

"My cousin has other interests outside of reading, but I keep hoping that perhaps one day I'll find the perfect novel that will entice her over to our way of thinking. She believes reading is dreadfully boring."

Lady Cranston laughed. "Then clearly she hasn't been reading the right books."

"I've told her as much, but it is difficult to convince her otherwise. It doesn't help that my aunt and uncle would never approve of the majority of what I read."

Hargrove chuckled. "But they did approve of the volume of poetry you borrowed?"

"Of course. They know nothing about Byron or they might have thought differently."

Lady Cranston smiled. "I think you might just have convinced me to give him a try."

The subject turned to the novels she'd read, and she was surprised to find that Hargrove had, indeed, read Ann Radcliffe's novel. She'd convinced herself that he was just being polite last week when he'd recommended it. It was one of those books everyone seemed to have heard of even if they'd never read it.

Eleanor caught the way Hargrove's sister kept glancing between the two of them, her curiosity evident, and tried to ignore it. She knew Hargrove's motivation in continuing their acquaintance was purely selfish.

For her part, she enjoyed his company. She might have envisioned him as the hero in more than one of the books she'd read, but she'd go to her grave before she admitted that fact. And if he did marry her cousin, they'd be seeing each other often. There was nothing untoward about her being on friendly terms with her cousin's husband.

Lady Cranston turned to her brother. "I think I need to sit for a few minutes. Would you mind terribly if I stay here while you finish?"

He took one of her hands and helped her to an overstuffed chair covered in green velvet. "Are you feeling unwell? We've been out too long. I'll ask for the carriage to be brought around to the front so you won't need to walk far."

Lady Cranston patted his hand before settling into the chair. "Nonsense. I just need to rest for a few minutes. Run along now. I'd like to get to know Miss Pearson better."

He frowned down at her from where he was standing next to her chair, and Eleanor knew he wanted to argue with his sister.

She settled into a seat. "I'll keep your sister company. If she begins to feel unwell, I'll come fetch you."

"I won't be long." He shook his head and looked at Lady Cranston. "If I overtire you, we both know your husband won't be pleased, and I'd rather not have his anger directed at me."

His sister laughed. "I'm always tired, so don't worry."

He glanced back at Eleanor before turning and exiting the reading room.

"I thought he'd never leave," his sister said. "You should call me Abigail since it seems we'll be getting to know one another."

Eleanor smiled. "Of course. And you may call me Eleanor."

Abigail examined her for several seconds before speaking again. "My brother likes you."

Heat flooded Eleanor's face, and she couldn't help feeling as though she'd been caught doing something wrong.

"Do you know about the connection between your brother and my… family?" If Hargrove's sister didn't know about the betrothal, Eleanor wasn't going to be the one to inform her. Not when an announcement wouldn't be made for several months yet.

Abigail nodded. "Yes, he told me about the"—she lowered her voice to a whisper—"betrothal."

Eleanor felt a measure of relief at the admission. She hated to think that Hargrove would have kept it a secret from his sister. "I am very close to my cousin. It would make matters quite uncomfortable if your brother *didn't* like me."

"I wish for my brother to find happiness when he marries. I don't know if that's possible if his hand is being forced."

Eleanor could understand the woman's concern, but it bothered her that Hargrove's sister seemed to be judging Lydia unfairly without having met her. "I can assure you that Lydia will make him a good wife."

Abigail tilted her head to one side. "And what of love?"

A pang of emotion Eleanor refused to name went through her. She had to take a deep breath before replying. "Love is something that happens in novels."

Abigail sighed. "I can assure you that isn't true. My husband and I love one another. I wish the same for my brother."

It was almost impossible to ignore how her heart was racing. "We can't all be so fortunate."

Abigail's scrutiny was beginning to make her feel uncomfortable. She didn't sense any maliciousness in it, but she couldn't help but wonder whether Hargrove's sister actually believed he was developing feelings for her. Not over Lydia, whom every other man wanted.

Abigail reached over and patted her on the hand. "I want to mention this before my brother returns. Please know that you are always welcome to call on me. I don't venture out often, but I can still receive visitors for at least two months before I enter my confinement."

Eleanor smiled. "Thank you. I'm surprised you're still receiving callers."

"Oh, we're not open to many. I find it annoying, but I do require quite a bit of rest. But we are always open to friends."

The words warmed Eleanor's heart. "Perhaps

after your confinement we can get to know one another better."

Abigail smiled. "I look forward to that. But if you ever need anything…" She glanced toward the door to the main bookstore. When she continued, her voice was just above a whisper. "If you ever need to contact my brother, you can do so through me. No questions asked."

Eleanor's thoughts scrambled at the implication. She was about to assure Hargrove's sister that would never happen when Abigail said, "Here he comes now."

When Hargrove reached them, his gaze moved over his sister. "How are you feeling?"

"I'm not about to collapse, Geoff. But the two of us have been having a delightful conversation about you."

Hargrove winced as he looked at Eleanor. "Don't believe anything she tells you."

Eleanor laughed, lightness filling her. It did something strange to her sensibilities to see him like this with his sister. It was so different from the stiff demeanor he portrayed whenever he was with Lydia, and she couldn't help but think that if her cousin ever saw this side of him, she would do everything in her power to capture this man's heart.

That thought shouldn't displease her, yet it did. It was an emotion Eleanor knew she had no right to feel. Lord Hargrove was friendly with her and had shown her a side to his personality that Lydia hadn't seen, but he could never be hers.

She tore her gaze from his, needing a moment to regain her equilibrium.

"So tell me, Eleanor, have you read *A Fallen Lady* yet?" Abigail asked.

"Oh yes, and it broke my heart. I'd been hoping for a happy ending."

An arch look entered Abigail's face. "The author is writing a sequel." She leaned closer and whispered, "It's to be titled *A Lady Redeemed*."

Eleanor's mouth dropped open. She'd heard nothing about another book. "How do you know that?" A thought struck her. No one knew who'd written the novel that had recently become a sensation. "Are you the author?"

Abigail shook her head. "Good heavens, no. But I might know who is. And no, I can't tell you. But I know she doesn't mind if people learn there's to be a sequel. Her publisher will be making an announcement soon to build anticipation."

"The author is a woman?"

Abigail shrugged. "Perhaps. Or I might be lying to throw you off."

Her gaze flew to Hargrove, who shrugged at her unasked question. "No, it isn't me. I may read novels, but I could never write one."

She narrowed her eyes on the man. "Do you know who it is?"

"No." He aimed a disapproving look at his sister. "My supposedly loving sister won't tell me."

Abigail glared at him in return. "Don't try to make me feel guilty. It isn't my secret to share. Besides, I'm fairly certain you have your own secrets you're keeping to yourself."

Hargrove and his sister both looked at her, and Eleanor was unable to keep the heat from rising to her cheeks.

She stood. "I should go choose my books now. It was a pleasure meeting you, Abigail." She turned to face Hargrove, who was watching her. "I wanted to thank you, my lord, for your generosity last week. It wasn't necessary but much appreciated."

He inclined his head. "It was a small thing, but I was glad to do it."

Their exchange hadn't done anything to stem her embarrassment. She dropped into a small curtsy and fled from the reading room, feeling two sets of eyes on her until she escaped into the bookstore.

She would need to temper her reaction to Lord Hargrove. It was clear that his sister realized she'd developed a tendre for the man. She'd have to be more careful.

Eleanor's eyes narrowed as she took in the concentration on her cousin's face while she played on the pianoforte. Lydia didn't like to sit still for Eleanor's drawings, but she didn't complain today when Eleanor suggested she draw her while she was practicing. She tried to memorize the way Lydia's mouth was flattened in a tight line, her eyes closed as she allowed the music to consume her.

When Lydia finished this song, Eleanor hoped she'd be able to convince her cousin to play another one so she could continue to draw. Lydia's patience with the task was already drawing to a close.

The final note hovered in the air, and Eleanor had just opened her mouth to make her request when Aunt Helen entered the room.

"I'm glad you're both here. I just received an invitation from Lord Hargrove for the two of you." She handed the note to Lydia, who was still seated before the instrument.

Eleanor tried to ignore the spark of delight she felt at being included in the invitation. She waited with impatience as Lydia's eyes scanned the paper. Then she walked over to Eleanor and handed it to her.

"You're going to be delighted, Ellie."

Eleanor took the note and glanced at the few lines. Her pulse was racing with excitement when she reached the end. "He wants us to attend the art exhibit at the Royal Academy."

"Should I tell him that the two of you would be delighted to accompany him?"

Aunt Helen knew Eleanor would never say no to the opportunity to visit Somerset House and view the painting exhibition. But her daughter was another matter.

Lydia let out a sigh. "Tell him that we would be delighted."

When Aunt Helen left the room, Eleanor went over to Lydia and hugged her. "Thank you."

Lydia hugged her back. "I'm sure it won't be horrible."

Two days later, Lord Hargrove called to collect them. Eleanor tried to contain her exuberance and allow Lydia to take the lead in their conversation during the short drive to Somerset House. Which meant that very little was said. Fortunately, Eleanor was saved from having to jump in and take over the conversation when the carriage slowed to a halt.

They'd driven by Somerset House before but had never gone inside. Eleanor was awed by its vast size. She was so excited she didn't even stumble when Lord Hargrove helped her down from the carriage.

She smiled her thanks and fell into step next to Lydia, who took Hargrove's arm.

Lord Hargrove had clearly been there before. He led the way with ease. "The climb up to the Great Room is steep, but I assure you the exhibit will be worth the effort."

Lydia was first onto the curved staircase. "Ellie has been looking forward to this since you sent the invitation. Did you know she draws? She's very talented."

"Is she?" He sent her a pointed look that she found impossible to decipher.

She tried not to think about it as she followed Lydia up the steep staircase. But when Hargrove moved into position behind her, she realized he now had an unimpeded view of her backside as they climbed the stairs. She imagined that she could feel the heat of his eyes on her the entire way up—really, she didn't think she'd ever climbed a staircase that had quite so many steps.

When they were almost at the top, she could no longer resist the urge to turn around and see what he was doing. She froze in place when she realized it hadn't been her imagination. He was staring at her backside!

He seemed to tear his eyes away, and when he met her gaze, there was a heat in their depths that unsettled her. And then he had the temerity to shrug.

With a small huff, she made her way up the last few steps to join Lydia, who was waiting for them.

But then Eleanor was struck speechless when she took in the Great Room.

It lived up to its name, being quite large, and the walls were impossibly high. And every inch of the walls was completely covered with paintings.

Curved windows lined the top of each wall providing plenty of light to showcase the art on display.

Eleanor let out a small gasp, and Lydia laughed.

Hargrove joined them. "I take that to mean you approve?"

She sighed. "Between Hatchards and now Somerset House, I don't know which is my favorite."

Lydia tucked her arm into hers. "Silly goose, you don't have to choose. I'm sure you'll be able to come back here again."

"Indeed," Hargrove said. "I'm rather fond of the exhibit myself."

Lydia let out a small gasp, and Eleanor glanced at her in alarm. "Is something the matter?"

Her cousin let out a small laugh that Eleanor knew was one she used when she was trying to affect an air of nonchalance.

"Of course not. Why would you say that? Come, Ellie, let us start here on this end of the room."

Lydia dragged her a few steps away from Hargrove and then tilted her head closer. When she spoke again, it was in a whisper. "Lord Stanley is here. Oh no, don't look. We mustn't be caught staring. He must come to us."

A thread of alarm went through her. This was all wrong. Lydia was supposed to be excited because she was here with Lord Hargrove and not because she'd spotted a different man.

"You're here as Lord Hargrove's guest."

"Yes, yes, of course. But promise me, Ellie. If Lord Stanley greets me, you must distract Lord Hargrove. Draw him away to talk about a painting on another wall. I'm sure you'll have no difficulty with that."

"Lydia…"

"We are in a public room. Look at all the people who are here! Nothing untoward will happen."

"I suppose you're correct."

Lydia squeezed her arm in reply, and together they turned to view the paintings before them. Eleanor found it impossible to concentrate, however, because Hargrove reached her side and stood much too close. And then Lord Stanley appeared beside Lydia.

"Miss Pearson," he said, a wide smile lighting up his face. "It is a pleasant surprise to see you."

Lydia aimed a smile at the man that had him puffing up with pride.

Eleanor glanced at Hargrove, wondering how he was taking this interaction. She half expected to find he'd be displeased, but the small, satisfied tilt to his lips told her that wasn't the case.

Lord Stanley held out his arm to Lydia. "I saw a very nice landscape painting I'd very much like to share with you."

"Oh of course, my lord. I adore landscape paintings."

Lydia released Eleanor's arm and took hold of Lord Stanley's without another look back at her or Hargrove. The two proceeded a slow ramble to the other side of the large gallery.

Eleanor was now alone with a very satisfied Lord Hargrove.

CHAPTER 12

*A*s one, they both turned to view the paintings nearest them. Eleanor's attention seemed fixed on the portraits, but Geoffrey's attention was focused on her. He watched her out of the corner of his eye as she took a step back to gaze at the paintings that were hung higher on the wall.

She'd glanced at him when Stanley had swooped in to usurp Lydia's attention. Had she expected him to be upset? He couldn't help but wonder how she'd react if she realized Stanley was only here because he'd let slip his plans for that afternoon. Honestly, the man was far too easy to manipulate.

He wondered how long she intended to ignore

him. He'd hoped she'd be braver. It was clear that neither he nor Lydia intended to continue with the betrothal. If Stanley continued his pursuit—and it was clear the man was smitten with Lydia Pearson—then there would be no reason he and Eleanor couldn't be friends.

Friends. He was fooling himself if he thought he only wanted friendship from this woman. In truth, he thought very highly of Eleanor Pearson. She was intelligent, witty, and very attractive. She didn't possess the delicate beauty of her cousin, but there was no denying the fact that Eleanor's appeal was no less distracting.

He realized, of course, that if his father hadn't arranged this betrothal, it was very likely they wouldn't have met. He might have seen her in passing, but he wouldn't have come to know her. Because of his father's need to control every detail of his children's lives, Geoffrey had been forced to meet the woman who tempted him to consider changing his plans to put off marrying for some time yet.

Eleanor continued to study the paintings before her, diligently giving each one careful consideration before moving on to the next while he studied her. Not overtly, of course, but he was acutely aware of the woman standing next to him. If he wasn't careful, everyone present would be able to see his interest in her.

"This is quite a lovely painting," she said finally, just when he'd given up hope that she would speak to him at all. "I especially enjoy the way the artist has captured the sunlight streaming through the trees and the way it is reflected on the grass below them."

He turned to look at her more fully. "You don't like me, do you, Miss Pearson?"

He was behaving like a cad for baiting her in this way, but he was tired of trying to figure her out. She'd been friendly enough toward him at Hatchards when they'd met on those two occasions, but on others, like today, she seemed to want to avoid him altogether. It galled him that she was making him doubt himself.

She swallowed and closed her eyes for a brief moment. When she answered him, she didn't meet his gaze. "I wouldn't say that."

He raised one brow. "Then what would you say?"

"Things would be much... *easier*... if you weren't quite so aloof with Lydia. Heaven knows you've spoken more to me than you have to the woman you're going to marry."

He frowned and then made an effort to smooth out his expression. "We've already had this discussion on more than one occasion. I don't wish to marry your cousin, so why would I go out of my way to endear myself to her?"

She sighed. "You need to try."

"Furthermore, I'm fairly certain your cousin has no illusions about the likelihood of our *arrangement* ending in marriage."

His voice was low, but to ensure their conversation wouldn't be overheard, he'd taken a step to the left, then another, away from the small group of people standing to their right. Fortunately they were chatting among themselves and weren't paying Eleanor and him any attention.

Eleanor gave her head a small shake. "I don't know why you're being so stubborn about this."

He took another step to the left and she followed, no longer focusing on the paintings. He wanted to smile but tamped down the urge lest he give away the hand he was currently playing. "I think we all know that Miss Pearson prefers the company of someone else to mine."

She glanced at the other side of the large room

to where Lydia was smiling up at Stanley. The pair was too far away for them to overhear their conversation. Lydia burst into giggles, and Stanley's expression could only be described as besotted. Neither of them were looking at the artwork.

Eleanor's gaze narrowed on him. "Did you tell Lord Stanley that we were going to be here today?"

Ah, this woman was far too clever for her own good. He didn't answer, but she must have seen the truth on his face.

"You are most vexing, my lord. When you issued this invitation, I'd hoped it was because you finally decided to make an effort to get to know Lydia. She's delightful, and everyone loves her."

He lifted one shoulder in an indifferent shrug. "She's pleasant enough."

Her lips pressed together in a line and she shook her head. "Why are you going out of your way to be so obstinate about this? I know you said you didn't know about the betrothal until after your father passed, but if you're acting this way to spite him, the man is long past caring what you're doing."

He let out a small huff of laughter. "Wherever he is, I can assure you that he cares."

Eleanor frowned. "Your father did you a service.

There are many women with larger fortunes who aren't as beautiful or caring as my cousin. You need to stop fighting this before you succeed in driving her away." She cast another worried glance over at where her cousin and Lord Stanley had moved to one of the upholstered benches and were sitting next to one another, their bodies turned toward each other, and chatting as though they were the only people in the room. Geoffrey felt like cheering the man on.

He considered his response for a moment before changing the subject. "You haven't answered my question."

Her brows drew together. "You asked me a question?"

"Why don't you like me?" He waited, watching the way her lips pressed together in a firm line.

"You weren't asking me a question. You were making a statement."

Her attempt to avoid answering amused him. "Now I'm asking you. Why don't you like me?"

She looked away, and he thought she wasn't going to reply. Finally she said, "You're pleasant enough."

He chuckled, enjoying the way this woman had

thrown his own words about Lydia right back at him.

She glanced at her cousin again, her frown turning into a slight scowl.

He took another step away from the small group of people, grateful the exhibit wasn't overly crowded. She took a corresponding step in the same direction.

It interested him that he had the ability to make her forget her duty even though she seemed intent on ensuring he fulfilled his. He wondered how far she would follow him and decided to inch his way toward the shadowy doorway tucked into the corner of the room. There were no large windows in that room, and he knew it wasn't considered part of the exhibit. The one other time he'd been here, he'd ducked into the room, curious about what treasures it might hide. It seemed to be a staging area of sorts, where statues and paintings were stored away.

"Your admission pains me since I like you a great deal."

Her mouth dropped open and she stared at him, clearly surprised by his admission. Then she pressed her lips together again and looked away. Color tinged her cheeks.

"I know this situation came as a surprise to

you, and I appreciate how nice you've been to me. But I wish you wouldn't tease me like that."

He stilled, staring down at her. Finally, when she met his gaze again, he continued. "I'm speaking in earnest. Given a choice between you and your cousin, I would much rather get to know you." They'd reached the doorway, and she was still moving with him.

She shook her head. "That is impossible. I might as well be invisible when Lydia is standing next to me."

A burst of anger went through him. He wanted to reach out and shake some sense into her. Instead, he moved into the darkened room.

There was a statue just inside the doorway, and he moved past it. He half expected to hear Eleanor sigh and return to her cousin's side.

She surprised him by following him into the room. "Did you not see the sign by the doorway? This room isn't part of the exhibition."

Her voice was low, and he imagined she thought they would be chastised by one of the exhibition's curators if they were caught. It hadn't even occurred to her that society would most definitely frown on their being caught together like this, alone, but not because this room was closed to the public.

He held one hand to his lips and stepped farther into the room. She followed. Dim light filtered into the room from the skylighted room next door, and he could see the way her brows drew together in confusion.

He stared into her eyes, infusing his words with as much sincerity as he could. "You are not invisible, Eleanor. I see you."

She inhaled an audible breath and held his gaze for several long seconds. Finally she shook her head and looked away. "I don't believe you." In a whisper she added, "Much as I wish I could."

They weren't alone, not really. The sound of distant voices reminded him of that fact. Still, he had to fight against the temptation to pull her into his arms and kiss her. "Please look at me, Miss Pearson. Eleanor."

She sucked in a breath at his use of her given name, and for a moment he thought she would flee. Instead, she did as he asked and met his gaze.

He stared down at her, fixated by her dark eyes. They seemed to draw him in, make him wonder what secrets she was hiding within their depths. In the darkened room, the brown of her eyes was indistinguishable from her pupils, making her eyes appear even larger in her pale face. The effect was striking, and he couldn't help but wonder what it would be like to make love to this woman.

Desire slammed into him with a bone-deep ache. He grasped his hands together behind his back to keep from dragging her into his arms and kissing her senseless. Anyone could wander into this room at any moment, and he wouldn't dishonor her in that way. Not when she was still so fixated on placing her cousin's happiness above her own.

"As I said, it is you I wish to know better, not your cousin. My father did do me a service, but not because he chose my future wife. His scheming did have one happy effect. It's given me the opportunity to get to know you."

She shook her head. "No—"

"And if I can convince your cousin to speak to her father about ending the betrothal, you should know that I would like to take that opportunity to become better acquainted with *you*."

She didn't move, but he saw her reflexive swallow in the way her throat tightened.

"You're trying to confuse me. Convince me to betray Lydia to get your own way in this."

She started to turn away, and he surprised

himself by reaching for her, stopping her with a hand on her elbow. She could have fled his light hold, but his touch had caused them both to freeze.

"Eleanor?"

He released her at the sound of Lydia Pearson's voice drifting through the doorway from the other room.

Eleanor turned to face him, tilting her chin up in a show of defiance. "I don't believe you. This is just another trick. If Lord Stanley doesn't lure my cousin away, you're probably hoping I can convince her to speak to her father. But you should know that I won't betray Lydia no matter how much you might tempt me."

She turned away and strode from the room, her pace even.

He waited some time before following, hoping to allay any suspicion that they'd been alone in this room together. A smile touched his lips as he considered her parting statement. Eleanor Pearson was tempted by him. He could work with that.

CHAPTER 13

*E*leanor vowed that she would have her emotions firmly in check the next time she saw Lord Hargrove. When they arrived at the ball—their third in the past week—she wouldn't immediately check to see whether he'd already arrived. She would interact with the other guests and she wouldn't spend her time anticipating dancing with the man.

It was more difficult than she'd thought possible. Especially when others seemed intent to mention him.

"Lord Hargrove is here," Lydia said shortly after their arrival.

Eleanor ignored the way her heart leaped at her cousin's innocent comment. "That's nice."

"I wonder if he'll ask you to waltz again. I'm saving that dance for Lord Stanley."

She wondered the same thing, but she wouldn't admit it. Lydia had already remarked on several occasions that Hargrove went out of his way to dance with her. "Perhaps they won't have a waltz tonight."

"Oh, I hope they do," Lydia said with a soft sigh.

Fortunately, the first of a long line of men approached her cousin then and asked her to dance, saving Eleanor from the uncomfortable subject.

She congratulated herself on her discipline when she didn't glance about the room to see whether she could spot Hargrove. Instead, she made her way over to the group of women with whom she regularly chatted while her cousin danced.

"There you are," Miss Stapleton said. "I've been waiting for your arrival."

At the age of thirty, Miss Stapleton was never asked to dance. She was at every event, however, because she had a younger sister who was searching for a husband.

Eleanor wondered at the enthusiastic greeting.

She settled into a chair by the woman. "Did I miss anything exciting?"

Miss Stapleton liked to keep track of all the dancing couples. If anyone was bold enough to dance twice with the same man, she would announce that it was clear they were now courting.

"Alas, nothing out of the ordinary. But I wished to speak to you about Lord Hargrove."

Eleanor was unable to keep from searching the dancing couples for the man. She had a sudden fear that she would find him dancing with someone. Thus far, he'd only danced with her or Lydia. The thought that he was now showing preference for another woman left her feeling unsettled.

"He isn't dancing," Miss Stapleton said. "Which is why I wanted to speak to you."

Eleanor forced her gaze back to the woman. It was an effort to keep her expression even as she spoke. "I don't know the man well."

"But he dances only with you and your cousin. It is a pattern that is repeated at every ball at which the three of you are in attendance."

Of course she'd noticed. "His father was a friend of my uncle's. Our two families are connected only because of that friendship."

The woman let out a sigh. "I'll admit that I'm

relieved to hear that. I'd worried that he might be courting your cousin."

Eleanor said nothing lest she betray the complicated situation surrounding Lydia and Lord Hargrove. And if she was being honest with herself, it rankled just a little that it hadn't occurred to this woman that Lord Hargrove might be showing an interest in Eleanor.

Miss Stapleton leaned closer. "My sister was hoping to attract his attention. Would it be possible for you to mention her as a possible dance partner the next time you speak to him?"

She couldn't deny the woman's request despite the fact she very much wanted to do so. Hargrove wasn't hers. Even if he did manage to free himself from his betrothal to Lydia, he wouldn't court Eleanor.

She searched out the woman's sister and found her dancing with a man twice her age. She winced. It was no wonder she was hoping to dance with Hargrove if that was the quality of suitors she was attracting. Still, Miss Stapleton's sister was rarely without a partner. Like Lydia, she danced most of the sets, sitting out only when she needed a break.

"It doesn't appear that your sister is lacking for partners."

The woman's sigh was louder, and Eleanor suspected that she'd annoyed the woman with her observation. No doubt she'd expected Eleanor to agree to make the introduction as soon as possible.

"This is her second season, and she hasn't shown an interest in any of the men who are pursuing her. I thought that it might be prudent to broaden her circle of acquaintances. And since Lord Hargrove is being very elusive…"

"It doesn't appear that he's searching for a bride." That much was true.

Miss Stapleton narrowed her eyes, and Eleanor wondered if she'd done a poor job of hiding her dismay at the idea of Hargrove courting her sister.

"Are you denying my request?"

Eleanor shook her head. "Of course not. I'll see what I can do. I was merely worried about how I would bring up the subject."

The woman smiled, her relief obvious. "You've always struck me as a skilled conversationalist. I'm sure you'll have no issue mentioning my sister to Lord Hargrove."

Eleanor's smile felt frozen as she accepted the compliment.

Miss Stapleton frowned. "Is something the matter? You don't look well."

Eleanor brought a hand to her temple, which was now throbbing with her very real dismay. "I fear that I have a headache. Are you finding it stuffy in here?"

The other woman patted Eleanor's arm. "I've attended a few events myself when I was feeling unwell. But such is our lot in life. Our needs will always be second to those of our charges."

The sympathy in the woman's gaze only served to worsen Eleanor's mood.

"Perhaps I should go out onto the balcony for a few minutes. The fresh air might help to clear my head."

"Oh of course, my dear. This set won't be over for some time yet. If your cousin comes to look for you before you return, I'll keep an eye on her."

Eleanor thanked her and made her way to the garden doors. When she exited, there were several other couples already there, chatting amiably. The sight only soured her mood further.

Seeking solitude, she moved to the far end of the balcony, away from the laughing, happy couples.

When she'd arrived in London with her cousin's family, she'd thought she'd come to terms with her lot in life. But something had changed in the past few weeks. And she knew exactly who was to blame.

Hargrove.

"Eleanor."

For a moment she thought she'd imagined his low voice, coming toward her from just beyond the steps that led into the garden. But then she heard it again, and she turned toward the sound and squinted.

Hargrove was standing at the very edge of the pool of light that spilled out into the gardens from the open ballroom doors. It was as though she'd conjured him merely by thinking about him.

She looked over her shoulder. There was only one other couple on the balcony now, and their backs were turned to her. Before she could change her mind, she slipped down the garden steps and went to him.

"I don't—"

He placed a finger over his lips, reminding her that she shouldn't speak lest they be discovered. Then he held out a hand.

She stared at it for several long seconds, considering whether it was prudent to take it. But she'd only be lying to herself if she thought even for a moment she wasn't going to follow him.

She placed her hand in his, her heart leaping at the way he smiled down at her, and allowed him to lead her farther into the darkened garden.

CHAPTER 14

It was a miracle that Eleanor had accepted his invitation. He'd expected her to shake her head and return to the ballroom.

He hadn't visited these gardens before, so he didn't know where he was leading her. But when he saw her slip out of the ballroom earlier, he'd seized on the opportunity to finally have a private moment with her.

"We shouldn't go far."

Her whisper had him smiling. He rounded a corner behind a row of hedges, keeping her behind him lest they run into someone. It wasn't his intention to compromise her, not when that infernal betrothal agreement was still in place.

Fortunately, this part of the garden was empty.

Even better, there was a small garden bench and he led her there.

The moon was out and bright enough to allow him to scan the area. There were mainly hedges here with a few rosebushes clustered in front of where they sat. He was relieved to see there were two other exits through which they could escape if anyone approached.

He turned to look at Eleanor, who was staring at him with a slight frown.

"Why are we here?"

He couldn't resist teasing her. "I called to you and you came. And here we are."

She narrowed her eyes the smallest amount, and he wanted to laugh.

He lifted one shoulder. "I saw you slip out into the garden. You seemed upset, and I wanted to make sure nothing was amiss."

"Did anyone see you follow me out? I should return—"

He still held her hand, and he stroked his thumb along her palm. His caress halted her protest.

"I went out through a different door. I wasn't sure I'd be able to intercept you before you returned, but I had to try. Will you tell me why you were so upset?"

She looked away and he waited. Finally she squared her shoulders and turned to face him.

"Miss Stapleton wanted me to introduce you to her younger sister."

He tried to put a face to the name. "Do I know her?"

"She's one of the women I socialize with while everyone else is dancing."

He realized whom she was speaking about. He also knew the woman's sister. It was true that they hadn't been introduced, but the young woman had literally bumped into him on two separate occasions. Then she'd stared up at him, no doubt expecting him to become infatuated with her on the spot.

"We haven't been formally introduced, but I do know of whom you speak."

Her jaw was clenched, but somehow she managed to say, "I can introduce you."

The sight of her obvious displeasure only served to cheer him. Clearly she didn't wish to do so, but Miss Stapleton must have extracted her promise.

He stretched his legs out in front of him. "There's no need."

Her tense posture eased somewhat. "Perhaps you can dance with her once."

He scoffed. "She has no lack of dance partners."

Eleanor frowned again. "It seems quite likely that Lord Stanley might offer for my cousin. It's clear that he's besotted with her, and I know she favors him above all her other suitors."

Relief bubbled through him. "It appears that way. I'm glad to hear that she would entertain his suit."

They sat together for almost a full minute without words. Eleanor was looking at the roses, and he was looking at her. Thoughts and emotions crowded within him. He wanted to get to know this woman better, but how could he approach the subject without offending her? Who knew when they would have another rare moment of solitude together. But would she even entertain a close acquaintance when he was still formally betrothed to her cousin?

"So if Lydia does agree to marry Lord Stanley and the agreement is broken, are you still set on avoiding marriage?"

He rubbed at an ache in his chest. The truth was that he couldn't answer her question. "I don't know."

Her gaze swung to meet his, her eyes wide.

"That's not what you said earlier. You told me that you had no intention of marrying for the next few years. What has changed?"

What indeed. "I hadn't planned on it, no. And finding out my father was forcing me to do his bidding even from the grave?" A haze of anger threatened to overtake him whenever he thought of his parent's manipulations. But he wouldn't allow those emotions to creep into this conversation. "I'm not actively searching for a wife, but I'm not totally against the idea. As long as it's a match of my choosing, of course."

She searched his gaze, no doubt trying to ascertain the veracity of his statement. But in her eyes, he could see the question she wanted to ask. She wanted to know if he'd found that woman. If perhaps it might be her.

She opened her mouth to ask the question but then pressed her lips together and looked away.

He was overcome with the urge to shake her. She was so intent first on seeing him wed to her cousin and then wanted to introduce him—albeit begrudgingly—to another younger woman. Why couldn't she entertain the possibility that maybe the two of them could have something more?

"Ask me your question, Eleanor." His voice was rough, betraying him.

She shook her head, and he was unable to stop from reaching for her. His hands were on her shoulders, and he turned her to face him.

Her eyes were wide with surprise. "What—?"

He lowered his head and kissed her. It was soft, tentative. He might be frustrated, but he wasn't a brute who would force his unwanted attentions on a woman.

She stiffened in his arms. He was just about to pull away when she softened and leaned into him. He wrapped his arms about her waist and deepened the kiss.

It was clear she was a novice at kissing, but she was also a fast learner. Within moments she was meeting his hungry kiss with equal fervor, her arms wrapping around his neck.

One hand moved to her breast, kneading her there, enjoying the soft moan that escaped her lips. Mad with lust, he trailed his fingers along her décolletage and reached into her bodice.

With a gasp she pulled away from him. Her pupils were dilated, her breathing harsh as she rose to her feet.

"What are you doing?" Her voice was rough

with the same emotion he was feeling. Lust. But he could also see her guilt.

He'd pushed too hard, taken things too far. He should have waited until after the betrothal was a thing of the past.

He took a step back, needing the distance from Eleanor's distracting scent to clear his head. He ran a hand through his hair. "You are the most vexing woman I have ever met."

They stared at each other for several seconds.

"I should return," she said. "I'll be missed if I remain away too much longer… if I haven't been already."

He nodded. "I'll show you the side entrance I used and then return through the garden doors. If anyone questions you about your absence, you can make an excuse about going to the retiring room. You'll need to pass by it before returning to the ballroom."

She nodded, and they walked side by side in silence. His hands were clasped behind his back so he wouldn't reach for her again.

Stanley had better offer for Eleanor's cousin soon. Geoffrey didn't know how much longer he'd be able to keep his distance from this woman.

CHAPTER 15

Her encounter with Hargrove left her feeling elated but she also couldn't help but feel a twinge of guilt. Despite what Lydia had told her yesterday evening, she and Hargrove were still betrothed. Eleanor shouldn't have returned his kiss.

She didn't know what to do, so she avoided him. Over the next two weeks, he was at every event they attended. A tall, imposing presence, his gaze following her wherever she went. And the worst part was that he wasn't even hiding his interest. If there was dancing, he came to claim her hand for the waltz. He didn't even ask, and she wouldn't have refused him if he had.

If Lydia noticed, she didn't care because she

was equally wrapped up in Lord Stanley. Eleanor wouldn't have been surprised to learn that the two men had formed a pact—divide and conquer the Pearson cousins.

Lydia came into her bedroom that night after they were both ready for bed. She did so every night, her conversation peppered with Lord Stanley and how handsome and chivalrous he was. They'd attended a rout that evening. The house party had been crowded and there hadn't been any dancing.

Lord Stanley had been by Lydia's side for most of the evening. Eleanor, of course, had been with them for most of the evening. Lord Hargrove hadn't been in attendance. She'd grown so used to seeing him every evening that his absence had unbalanced her. She'd missed him.

Lydia sat on the edge of Eleanor's bed and watched her as she plaited her hair before turning in for the night. Eleanor studied her cousin's reflection in the dressing table mirror.

Lydia took a deep breath before saying, "I'm going to speak to Father tomorrow about breaking the betrothal."

Eleanor's heart leaped at the statement. It had become clear that things between her cousin and Lord Stanley were headed in this direction, but she hadn't expected the betrothal to end this early in the season. It was only April.

She turned on the bench and faced her cousin. Her hands were shaking, so she gripped them in her lap. "I would be very happy to lend my support when you speak to him."

Lydia shook her head, and a wide smile lit her face. "Lord Stanley will be calling tomorrow afternoon to ask his permission to marry me. If I'm to be a marchioness one day, I'm going to need to start doing these things on my own."

Eleanor crossed the room and sat next to her cousin on the bed. She wrapped her in a tight hug. "I'm very happy for you. I'm sure Uncle will be happy as well. Lord Stanley is a good man, and he seems devoted to you."

Lydia's arms tightened on her before she pulled back. "Lord Hargrove will be happy. I know that you're fond of him and hoped that we'd make a match, but…" She shrugged.

It was difficult for Eleanor to keep her expression neutral. Just thinking about Hargrove had her emotions in turmoil. "He was always very nice to you."

"He was, but I don't think he ever saw me as a woman." There was a twinkle in her eye when she added, "He never looked at me the way he looks at you."

Eleanor couldn't hold back her blush. "We're on friendly terms, nothing more."

Lydia reached for her hands and squeezed them. "Yes, Ellie, it is. You are very beautiful. I know I'm spoiled, but you've always been nothing but kind and generous to me. You've never been jealous when men approached me."

Eleanor shrugged. "It is what it is. I am passably attractive, but no one would ever prefer me to you. It makes sense that men are drawn to you."

"No. Ellie, you are beautiful—both inside and out. There is more than one type of beauty, and it is quite obvious to me that Lord Hargrove appreciates your beauty more than mine."

"I think…" She had to take a deep breath to settle her nerves before she continued. She wasn't used to being the subject of conversation when she and Lydia were discussing suitors. "We are friends."

Lydia tilted her head to one side. "I think you could be more than friends."

Eleanor shook her head, unable to hold back a wave of sadness. "He doesn't wish to marry."

"He doesn't wish to marry *me*. I'm not sure the same holds true for the two of you."

Eleanor stood, needing this conversation to be at an end. "I don't want you to concern yourself about me."

Lydia let out a soft breath. "And that, my dear cousin, is the problem. You no longer need to worry about me and what my future holds. I've found a man that I love. There is no reason we can't both be happy."

"When are you planning to tell your father? I am, as always, at your service if you need me for emotional support afterward."

Lydia shook her head, and it was clear she knew Eleanor was trying to change the subject. Fortunately, she didn't press the matter. "I'll speak to him tomorrow at midday. Lord Stanley will be arriving before we normally receive callers. He plans to ask for my hand then." She dimpled. "I thought it might be best for Father to agree to end my betrothal to Lord Hargrove before he arrives."

"I'm so happy for you," Eleanor said. "Everything has worked out just as it should. Lord Hargrove isn't going to press his suit, you've had the glorious season you wished for, and you've fallen in love."

Lydia's gaze softened. "Now that my future will be settled, you need to start worrying about yourself. I won't be upset if something was to transpire between you and Lord Hargrove." An arch look entered her eyes. "Also, I was thinking that you should be the one to tell Lord Hargrove."

Eleanor shook her head. She couldn't. "Perhaps Uncle—"

"No," Lydia said with a shake of her head. "The news should come from you. That way you'll see his reaction firsthand. That will tell you how he feels about you. Will he want to wipe his hands of this entire matter and move on, relieved he's getting what he wanted from the beginning? Or will he let you know that he wants to pursue you?"

Her words echoed within Eleanor's heart. Lydia stood and gave her another hug before sweeping from the room and she watched her go in amazement. When had her younger cousin become so wise? It appeared that finding true love had given Lydia a maturity that Eleanor hadn't expected to see for several more years.

Lydia was correct—she should be the one to tell Hargrove.

Excitement began to thrum through her. Surely the friendship that had begun to develop between them was real. And unless he was a consummate actor, he wanted more than friendship from her.

Not marriage, of course. Hargrove had been very clear about not wanting to marry. But there was no reason Eleanor couldn't have a taste of what it would be like to be with him as more than friendly acquaintances. She was five and twenty. Older women conducted discreet affairs of the heart, and society looked the other way. It was possible that she and Hargrove could have a similar understanding.

Her heart wanted more, of course, but in this she would allow her head to rule. They didn't have a future together, but they could enjoy this brief moment in time. There were still three months ahead of them before the season was over.

Her heart was racing with anticipation as she crawled under the covers.

CHAPTER 16

It was early afternoon when Geoffrey received a message from his sister asking him to visit as soon as possible. The summons triggered his concern, and he raced from the house. Her baby wasn't due for another month, so it was still a little early. Even worse, women died in childbirth. If she was on her deathbed, he knew she'd call for him.

A footman had scarce opened the door when he rushed inside. "Is she upstairs?"

His sister's laughter coming from the drawing room had him scowling. He took a deep breath to calm his racing heart and followed the sound. His gaze went immediately to the armchair she liked to use of late because she needed the support of the chair's arms to rise.

His eyes moved over her face before dropping to her belly. She hadn't given birth. He folded his arms across his chest. "Your note said I needed to come right away. I thought you were…" He waved a hand over her midsection.

"I am quite well, Geoff. How are you today?"

The sound of muffled laughter had him turning his head to the settee. He froze when he realized Eleanor was there.

"We have an unexpected but very welcome guest," his sister said.

He turned to look at her. "We?"

She nodded. "Miss Pearson needed to speak to you, but since she couldn't call on you, she came here instead."

He noticed the blush on Eleanor's cheeks, and it made her even more attractive to him. They stared at one another for several long seconds before he collected his wits. He wanted to ask her a million questions but couldn't. Not with his sister in the room. Instead, he inclined his head in greeting. "Miss Pearson."

Abigail let out a loud sigh. "Come help me up, Geoff."

He moved to do so automatically, his thoughts still racing. What could have happened that would have Eleanor seeking him out in this manner? They saw each other each week at the bookstore. She could have waited to speak to him there.

Eleanor stood as well. "I hope this wasn't an inconvenience." She winced. "Of course it was. I shouldn't have bothered you."

Abigail squeezed her hand. "Nonsense. I'm glad to be of service. But if the two of you will excuse me, I need to leave you for a little while." She placed a hand over her swollen midsection, caressing the bump. "I think the two of you need to have this conversation in private."

She dropped a kiss on his cheek, using the opportunity to whisper into his ear and press something into his hand. "I sent her coach away with a note that I would require her assistance for the next few hours. This is the key to my old town house. We haven't had the opportunity to do anything with it yet, and it occurs to me that you might find a use for it." She winked at him and mouthed, "There will be no one there."

He slipped the key into a pocket and watched her leave. When they were alone, he turned to face

Eleanor. They stared at one another. Finally she sank down onto the settee with a loud sigh.

He didn't think twice before sitting next to her. They so rarely had the opportunity to be alone together, and he needed to be as close to her as possible.

When she didn't speak, he broke the silence. It must have taken much courage to reach out to his sister today, but now he feared Eleanor might change her mind. "You wanted to speak to me?"

Eleanor shifted so she was facing him. "I have news about my cousin and Lord Stanley."

He stilled, hoping that the next words out of her mouth was that the two would be marrying. That would be the best outcome to their current situation, but Lord Appleby seemed quite insistent that a match be made between their two families. It wasn't outside the realm of possibility that Eleanor's uncle had put an end to Stanley's courtship.

"And what is that news?"

Eleanor's eyes seemed to search his. Her chest rose as she took a deep breath, but somehow he kept his gaze on her face. "She has accepted his suit. She is speaking to my uncle today and has high hopes that he'll allow her to break your betrothal."

The relief he felt was overpowering. He closed

his eyes for a moment, trying to hold back his desire to cheer. But he didn't hold back the smile that spread across his face as he opened his eyes again.

Eleanor was still watching him carefully, as though she was trying to read his thoughts. Did she think he would thank her and then take his leave? He would have done just that two months ago at the beginning of the season. Now everything had changed.

He reached for her hand and held it. They both wore gloves, but a thrill of anticipation surged through him. There was nothing stopping him from getting to know this woman better.

"I won't lie. You know I'm beyond thrilled to hear that." Finally Stanley's sense of competition had come in handy. Never had Geoffrey been so glad to have the man best him.

Her voice was soft when she said, "I know."

Eleanor's tongue flicked over her lips, and he wanted to groan. He wanted to pull her into his arms, onto his lap, but he couldn't rush her. She'd returned his kiss last night in the garden, but now he wanted so much more from her.

"What...?" Again with that infernal licking of her lips that was tempting him beyond reason. "What are you planning to do with your freedom?"

He looked down at their clasped hands, where his thumb had been tracing circles on the back of hers. He lifted her hand to his mouth and placed a kiss on the smooth skin of her wrist, above where the fabric ended. Her scent—roses, if he wasn't mistaken—was stronger there.

At her sharp intake of breath, he met her eyes. "I'd like to get to know you better."

She stared at him, her expression impassive for several interminable moments before she smiled. "I was hoping you'd say that. I've been feeling so guilty about my… attraction to you."

His voice lowered and he leaned in closer. "You're attracted to me?"

She let out a small huff of laughter and pulled her hand from his. "You know I am. You've been doing everything in your power to charm me. I know it's because you were hoping to get me on your side with respect to my cousin—"

"No," he said with a frown. "Well, perhaps at first. But you must know that I've come to think highly of you. And I wasn't lying about my own attraction."

Truer words had never been spoken. This woman had begun to bedevil him. Marriage wasn't something he'd expected to contemplate for several more years, but something about Eleanor Pearson had him thinking he needed to consider the matter now. Before someone else snatched her up.

A flicker of emotion crossed her face. "I…" She shook her head and turned away from him.

He moved closer to her. They weren't touching, but it was a near thing. Somehow he resisted the urge to reach for her chin and turn her face back to him. "Tell me."

She took another deep breath and turned to look at him. "I am five and twenty."

She seemed to think those words should convey something to him, but he found himself at a loss as to their significance. "And?"

"No one is going to offer me marriage."

He couldn't hold back his laugh.

She folded her arms across her chest and frowned. "I'm happy to see my current life circumstances bring you such amusement."

He sobered but couldn't keep from smiling at her ridiculous statement. "If one thing is clear to me, it is that you are devoted to your cousin. And heaven knows her parents spoil her."

She opened her mouth to interrupt, but he continued. "I'm not saying anything negative about Miss Pearson, only that it is clear you have all placed her needs above your own. Especially you. But once she's wed, you'll be free to look to your own future."

She shook her head. "I'll still be far too old."

"Eleanor." He loved the way her name rolled off his tongue. "My sister is twenty-seven, and she is with child. There is still time for you to have a family of your own."

He couldn't shake the image of her rounded with child. The thought caused an unexpected yearning, but he pushed the feeling aside. It was far too soon for him to be thinking about children. He still had to decide whether he wanted a wife.

One corner of her mouth lifted, but her words were tinged with a hint of bittersweet emotion. "That might be true, but we both know that men seek out women who are Lydia's age, not mine. No one is going to look at me, even without Lydia by my side."

He wanted to shake her. Why was she being so stubborn about this? "I'm looking at you."

She met his gaze. "But not as a wife. We both know you have no intention of marrying. Not yet."

He had to ignore the urge to deny her assertion. In truth, he no longer knew what he wanted. He was relieved to be free of his unwanted betrothal, yes. But surely he wasn't considering turning around and proposing to another woman. He was confused and needed time to think.

"I have come to terms with my reality. But that doesn't mean…"

She looked away, and Geoffrey found himself hanging on to her words. She stiffened her spine and turned to face him again. This time it was Eleanor who reached for him and entwined their fingers. Heated awareness coursed through his body and he knew—*he knew*—what she was going to say.

"That doesn't mean I don't want to know what it would be like to be with a man. Women my age can take lovers. Society looks the other way."

His pulse was racing. "Would your aunt and uncle look the other way?"

She let out a surprised laugh. "Heavens no. But once Lydia is married, I will no longer be called upon to chaperone her. I will have a measure of freedom."

The key his sister had given him was a heavy weight in his pocket. Abigail had known what would happen between him and Eleanor. That he would want to make her his.

"Eleanor."

She swallowed. "Yes, my lord?"

"I'm going to need to hear the words from you. Why am I here? Your uncle could have told me about the broken betrothal himself. And more importantly, why are you telling me about your plans for the future?"

She stared at him for almost a full minute. He waited. Embarking on a physical affair would be no small thing for Eleanor, not if she was as innocent as he suspected. He'd pursued her, yes. He'd crossed several lines that would have people gossiping about the two of them if they were discovered. But he wouldn't push her on this. He wanted... No, he *needed* this decision to be hers.

"I want to have a discreet affair with you."

Affair. Not love affair, which he would have thought she'd want. Somehow that thought bothered him.

"And if I refuse you? Would you find someone else?"

Her mouth dropped open in shock. Did he actually believe she would— nay, that she *could*—make this same proposal to another man?

She tried to pull her hand from his grip as she rose to her feet, but he refused to release her. Instead, he followed and stood far too close for her sensibilities. Their fingers were still entwined.

Heat colored her cheeks. "Never mind. I am sorry to have bothered you with this request. Since you now have the freedom you wanted, I beg you to release my hand and do the same for me."

His gaze remained fixed on her face. "You haven't answered my question."

Why was he being so infuriating? "If you must

know, the answer is no. I have no intention of approaching another man."

His mouth curled up with a smirk of satisfaction that had her temper spiking. That could be the only reason she added, "But one never knows what the future may hold."

She let out a small yelp when he tugged her hand, setting her off-balance, and she collided with his chest. His other hand splayed across her upper back, holding her against him.

She met his intense gaze, and for a moment she forgot to breathe. She'd seen desire in his gaze before, when he'd kissed her. But that was nothing to the heated fervor within the blue depths of his eyes now. She was unable to move, trapped by whatever was happening between them.

"Wrong answer," he said.

Good heavens. Hargrove's voice was a low growl that sent shivers of awareness through her body. "What—" Her voice broke on the question. She had to lick her lips and swallow before she could continue. "What is the correct answer?"

He pressed her even closer to him. The feel of his arousal was unmistakable. "The correct answer is that you want only me."

His mouth crashed down on hers in a bruising

kiss, and she opened immediately to receive him. Her legs felt weak, and if he hadn't been holding her against him, she feared she would have swooned.

The kiss was over far too soon, but Hargrove didn't release her.

She blinked up at him, her thoughts muddled, and then pressed her face against his chest. A shudder went through her. Finally, after taking a deep breath, she pulled away from him.

"We can't do this here," he said as he released her, his arms dropping to his side.

She felt the loss of his embrace acutely. Trying to hide her embarrassment, she aimed for levity. "You were the one who kissed me."

One corner of his mouth lifted, and the heat in his gaze had her stomach swooping.

"I'd like to do more than kiss you." Impossibly, his voice had dropped even lower.

She was incapable of thought. He'd rendered her speechless. "I…"

He laughed, the sound light. "I'd very much like to accept your offer."

"So would I," she repeated, caught up in the heightened awareness that seemed to be swirling around them.

He gazed at her, clearly amused at her inability to form a coherent thought. She was completely out of her depth and would have to rely on him as to how to proceed.

She cleared her throat. "How?"

"I'll escort you to my carriage and then speak to my driver. He'll take you to my sister's town house. The one in which she resided before she married." He pressed a key into her hand. "The house will be empty. Wait for me."

This was happening so much faster than she'd anticipated. She should be terrified at the mere thought of taking such an irrevocable step with this man. If anyone learned about their affair, she would be ruined.

But she didn't care. She wasn't looking for a husband. Yes, there had been a few gentlemen over the past few years who'd expressed interest in courting her, but she'd turned them all away. Her first duty had been to Lydia.

Now though, who knew what the future would hold? Many already considered her too old to marry. She'd come to terms with the fact that she'd waited too long and was now destined to be a spinster. But while she didn't regret turning away any of those men, she would regret losing this opportunity with Hargrove.

She clutched the key and nodded. When he offered her his arm, she took it and followed him to his carriage.

CHAPTER 18

*S*eated within the comfort of Hargrove's carriage, Eleanor considered his last words to her before he closed the door. *If you change your mind, ask the driver to take you home.*

His concern for her, even when it was clear he very much wanted her to proceed to Abigail's former home, only served to convince her she'd made the right choice.

Still, she took the time to search her heart for even a hint of doubt. There was no denying she was nervous. She knew what to expect, but knowing and experiencing were two different things. But she could no longer escape the truth of her feelings for Lord Hargrove. Even if they could never be together, she wanted to experience the act of inti-macy with a man she loved.

She hadn't wanted to admit her feelings while he was still betrothed to her cousin, but now they were both free. More importantly, Lydia had given her blessing. Not that her cousin expected Eleanor to engage in a love affair with the man, but Lydia was young and she was a romantic. Eleanor was more practical.

Calm had settled over her by the time the carriage reached its destination. Eleanor thanked the carriage driver, who had come around to help her down, and made her way into the small brick town house.

The silence seemed to echo around her as she closed the door behind her. She didn't know whether Hargrove had another key, so she left the door unlocked.

She turned right into what was clearly the drawing room. The house was still furnished, but a fine layer of dust had settled on most of the surfaces. It was a welcome sight because it meant there would be no servants intruding on their privacy. Looking at her, judging her. And there would be no danger that gossip might make it back to her uncle's household.

She settled into an armchair to wait. Fifteen minutes passed before she heard someone at the front door. She rose, only then realizing that perhaps it would have been better to hide. What if someone else also had access to this house?

She almost sagged with relief when Hargrove appeared. Their gazes locked.

He entered the room. "You're here."

"You thought I'd change my mind?"

He closed the distance between them. He was within arm's reach when he stopped. She wanted to throw herself into his arms, but uncertainty about how to proceed had her remaining frozen in place.

"I didn't believe you would, but one can never be certain."

He lifted a hand, and she placed her ungloved hand in his without hesitation. She'd removed her gloves while waiting for him. Given what was about to happen, it seemed silly to insist on the formality of keeping her hands encased within the white linen. "You can be sure about me."

He brought her hand to his lips, his eyes lighting with what could only be called devilish delight before he flipped her hand over and pressed a kiss onto her palm. Shock raced through her when she felt the tip of his tongue.

"I look forward to tasting you all over," he murmured, his breath coasting along the small wet patch and increasing her skin's sensitivity.

"Good heavens. Now I understand why we're admonished to keep our gloves on while in the presence of a gentleman."

He barked out a surprised laugh. Keeping her hand firmly in his, he turned and led her from the room and up to the second floor of the house. With every step, anticipation grew within her until it was a living, breathing thing. The shocking feel of his tongue on her hand had her wondering how it would feel elsewhere on her body.

She took a deep breath and pushed back those thoughts. This first time was going to hurt. Would there be another? Perhaps she should have asked him what would happen afterward, but she found that she didn't care. Whether they would be together once or several times over the remainder of the season, she still wanted to be with him.

She glanced sideways at him when he stopped before a door and looked inside. With a shake of his head, he took her with him and repeated his actions until he found the room he was looking for.

He didn't bother to close the bedroom door

after they entered the room. There was no need since no one was here.

Hargrove dropped her hand and turned to face her, his eyes dark with emotion. "If I were a true gentleman, I'd give you one more opportunity to change your mind."

She took one step closer. Mere inches separated them. "If I were a proper lady, I wouldn't be here."

Seconds stretched as the air became heavy. He stared down at her. Somehow she knew what he wanted without having to hear the words. He was waiting for her to make the first move.

She closed those last few inches, leaned into his body, and wrapped her arms around his neck to bring his head down to hers. With a groan, he held her against him and kissed her, his mouth moving against hers with heated urgency.

She gave in to the desire rising within her and returned the kiss. Gone were the last of her inhibitions. She was free from any lingering guilt concerning her cousin and was an eager participant. Hargrove had more knowledge than her when it came to conducting affairs, but she vowed to be an eager pupil and follow his lead.

Her hands shifted to the shoulders of his tailcoat, and she pushed the fabric down his arms and removed it.

She stilled as she stared at him. She'd seen her uncle wearing just a waistcoat and shirt, but it was far more intimate to be standing in a bedroom with Hargrove while he was similarly dressed.

"You don't pad your coat." She knew that many men did to make their shoulders appear broader. Her uncle was one of them.

She lifted a hand to his shoulder, delighting in the feel of the muscles there, before also feeling his arm. When she brought her hand to his chest, he captured it in his and held it imprisoned against his heart.

With a small shake of his head, he took the coat she was still holding over one arm and moved to the dressing table, where he laid it on its surface.

She could only stare, frozen in place, as he removed his cravat and waistcoat. The spell was broken when he placed those items over his coat and turned to face her again, one brow raised.

Heat colored her cheeks at the way he'd caught her ogling him. But it was impossible to believe she was actually in this room, watching him disrobe. That they were going to make love.

Embarrassment spurred her into action even as

she realized she wasn't behaving rationally. Hargrove must know she found him attractive.

Her dress had tiny buttons all the way down the back, and she wouldn't be able to undo them herself. She squared her shoulders, trying to mimic his air of confidence when it came to disrobing in front of another.

"I'm going to need your assistance, Hargrove."

A slight grimace crossed his face, and she took a step back. Had she already muddled things? "I apologize, my lord—"

"No." He closed the distance between them again. "I don't want this formality between us. It's just that hearing you use my title now, when we're about to make love…" A small frown creased his brow. "It hasn't been that long since my father died. Every time someone calls me by his title, I expect to see him walk into the room."

His gaze settled on hers as though it were vital to him that she believe him. "The very last thing I want to think about right now is my father."

She nodded in understanding. Their relationship had been strained, so what he'd said made sense. "What should I call you?"

"My given name is Geoffrey."

He cupped her cheek, and she turned her face

to place a kiss on his palm before smiling up at him. "I'd tell you to call me Eleanor, but you've been doing that for some time now."

He laughed, the corners of his blue eyes crinkling. She loved his eyes.

He spun her around and began undoing the long row of buttons. With each one, her anticipation grew. When her dress was loosened, he spread the fabric and dropped a kiss on her shoulder. She shuddered at the heat of his breath on her skin.

Finally, after slipping the last button loose, he took a step back. She turned to face him, her hands the only thing holding the dress in place. She watched his face as she dropped her arms and allowed the material to fall into a puddle on the floor.

CHAPTER 19

It was now his turn to stare. His eyes raked up and down her form where she stood, wearing only her white chemise and corset. Somehow he kept from throwing her onto the bed and having his way with her. This was going to be their first time together—the first of many if he had any say in the matter. He didn't want to scare her by rushing.

"Take down your hair." His voice was rougher than normal, and he couldn't say why. He'd bedded other women, but there was something about Eleanor that affected him in a way no one else had.

She raised her hands to do that, and his eyes glided down to take in the way her breasts threatened to spill over the top of her stays.

Clenching his fists at his side, he forced himself to watch her remove the pins. When she was done, she released the heavy mass of dark hair. It fell past her shoulders and covered the tops of her breasts.

She walked over to the dressing table and scattered the pins on its surface next to his clothing. She left her dress on the floor, almost as though she'd forgotten about it. He bent to retrieve it and draped it over the dressing table's bench seat. She wouldn't want to return home and have anyone ask why her dress was wrinkled.

She was within arm's reach but hadn't turned to face him. Before she could ask for assistance, he began to unlace her corset. Her breaths were coming in shallow pants now, telling him just how much his nearness affected her.

When he removed the corset, she let out a sharp exhale of relief but didn't turn to face him. He wanted to pull down her chemise but resisted the temptation. Going slowly might just kill him.

He pulled her against him, wrapped his arms around her waist, and pressed his mouth against her neck. "Never doubt that you are beautiful, Eleanor."

He hated that she saw herself as inferior to her cousin. Lydia's beauty was delicate, and he didn't enjoy the idea of being with a woman who reminded him of a fragile porcelain figurine. He preferred real women who didn't look like they would break.

He urged his hardness against her hip and she gasped. Good. He wanted her to know exactly what she was doing to him.

Moving with a patience he hadn't thought he possessed, he took her hand and led her to the bed. When she sat on its edge, he stepped back to remove the rest of his clothing. Her stare was a physical caress over his body. He was harder than he'd ever been, his need a desperate ache, but he allowed her to look her fill as he stood before her.

He groaned when she wet her lips, thoughts flooding him about just where he wanted to feel that tongue. She leaned away from him when he lowered himself to sit next to her.

One corner of his mouth tilted up. "I hope that doesn't mean you're reconsidering?"

She gave a small laugh. "I find myself feeling shy around you now that you're…"

"Naked?"

"Without clothing."

This time he laughed as he shifted and lay down on top of the bedsheets. "Will you be joining me?"

She covered her face with her hands, and for one terrifying moment, he feared she was going to bolt. "Eleanor?"

She dropped her hands, her expression serious. "Can I keep my chemise on? I don't think I have the courage to disrobe completely."

He offered her his hand. "Of course."

With a deep breath, she placed her hand in his and allowed him to tug her onto the bed next to him. They lay on their sides, facing one another. Him without a stitch of clothing on, Eleanor wearing her chemise. He waited for her to speak first.

"I'm so happy that Lydia found someone else. I dreaded the fact that you would one day be my cousin's husband."

He stroked the back of his hand along her jaw, up the side of her face, and then buried his fingers in her hair. "I don't know how I would have survived being near you and not being able to have my way with you."

He lifted himself over her, hovering with his weight braced on his forearms. Then he lowered himself so he could feel the soft curves of her body under his. Desire spiked within him.

CHAPTER 20

Geoffrey's bare body against hers caused a tumult of sensation that threatened to overwhelm her. The heat of his body, his skin touching her all along her length, burned even through the fine lawn of her chemise. But above everything, she was acutely aware of the hard length of him pressing into her thigh. She was incapable of speech.

"I hate that making love to you will hurt you, but I'll make sure you find your pleasure first."

She was already finding a great deal of pleasure—she didn't know how it could be better. "I trust you."

He kissed her, his mouth eager and hungry on hers. She returned the kiss with a passion she didn't know she was capable of feeling. The more he asked of her, the more she wanted to give him.

His mouth moved along her jaw to her neck, and she tilted her head to give him better access. She arched into his hand when he cupped her breast and held her breath as his mouth trailed lower. He'd touched her breasts before, that evening in the garden, but now she needed to feel his mouth on her. He kissed all around first one breast, then the other. She buried her fingers in his hair, hoping to direct his mouth to her nipples, which were aching. Instead, he chuckled and lifted his head to meet her gaze.

"Is there something in particular you want me to do?"

She wanted to growl in frustration, but a part of her was amazed at his teasing tone. She'd never imagined that physical intimacy could be fun. "You know what I want."

"Maybe I need to hear you say it."

Her mouth dropped open. "Out loud?"

His eyes danced with amusement. "Yes, Eleanor. With actual words."

She bit her lip as she considered her current dilemma. She'd never imagined he'd actually want her to tell him what to do. Not when she didn't know anything beyond the basics about what it meant to be with a man. But she did know this one thing. He'd shocked her when he'd touched her bare breast before. She wasn't capable of shocking him, but she could prove herself an eager partner in their lovemaking.

"I want your mouth on me here." She circled a nipple with a finger, enjoying the way his eyes fixated on her hand. Heady power coursed through her as she moved her hand to her other breast. "And then here."

There was no more teasing. He lowered her chemise until her breasts were bared and then drew her nipple into his mouth, pulling hard on the stiffened peak. Heat shot down her belly, straight to her core.

She clung to his head, keeping him there, enjoying the wicked pleasure that coursed through her.

She mourned the feel of his mouth on her when he raised his head, but she'd known this part was coming. He wouldn't be able to make love to her with just his mouth. But instead of moving to cover her again, he began to kiss her belly over her chemise.

"Geoffrey?"

"Shh, let me prepare you."

She felt his hand on her thigh, and then he was raising the material of her chemise. Her breath lodged in her throat when he pulled it above her hips, exposing her sex. She gasped when he touched her there with his fingers.

He groaned as though he were in pain. "You're already wet for me."

Then he moved even lower and settled between her thighs.

A hint of alarm raced through her. "I don't understand—"

Her mind blanked when he spread her legs farther apart and brought his mouth there, between her legs. She lost her ability to speak when he began to pleasure her with his mouth, slipping in one finger that moved within her body in imitation of the act she knew would be coming.

This felt far more wicked than making love, but Eleanor didn't protest. She couldn't because she enjoyed it far too much. She'd never imagined that such intimacies could take place between a man and a woman in the bedchamber.

She broke apart with a harsh cry, an unbearable wave of pleasure racing through her.

Geoffrey's grin was devilish when he surged into place above her.

She traced his lips with a finger. "Propositioning you was the best idea I've ever had."

"I heartily concur." And then he was pressing into her. He was so much bigger than the finger he'd had in her body, and for a moment she feared he wasn't going to fit. Finally, with one powerful surge, he was inside her.

He stilled, and she knew he was allowing her to adjust to the feel of his invasion. She was grateful because it hurt. The pain wasn't excruciating—she'd actually expected it to be worse—but it was uncomfortable. And there was a slight sting.

He kissed her, his mouth moving slowly over hers. She loved kissing him and found herself taking the lead, deepening the kiss by pressing her tongue into his mouth with a moan.

She couldn't say how long they continued to kiss, but all too soon he lifted his head and stared down at her. His jaw was clenched, his eyes almost black.

She knew what he was thinking. He wondered if he should continue or if he should pull out. Her maidenhead was gone, and the next time they made love it wouldn't hurt. Or so she'd been told.

But she didn't want him to stop. The pain had subsided, and she found she was greedy for more. She wrapped first one leg, then the other, around his hips. "Make love to me."

And heavens how he did, moving within her with powerful, steady strokes. It was too much. Everything they'd shared, the release he'd already given her with his mouth. She found herself screaming out her pleasure all too soon, her body convulsing against his hard length as he continued to move within her. With a soft curse, he pulled out of her warmth and spent himself outside her with a guttural moan.

They stared at one another for several long moments, him suspended above her, their breaths coming in harsh pants.

Then he shifted their positions so he was lying on his back and she was draped across his chest.

She snuggled against him and allowed herself the luxury of enjoying this moment. Hopefully it would be the first of many, but if her parents' deaths had taught her anything, it was that the future could never be predicted. No matter how well one thought they'd planned for it.

CHAPTER 21

*A*ll too soon it was time for them to dress and return to their regular lives. Eleanor hated having to leave Geoffrey, but he'd promised there would be much pleasure ahead for the two of them.

Geoffrey arranged for his carriage driver to take her home, but he didn't join her. They couldn't be seen together. That thought left her feeling a twinge of sadness, but she refused to dwell on it.

Her spirits were still high when she entered the town house on Grosvenor Square. One glance at her cousin, who rushed out of the drawing room, her brow wrinkled with concern, had her expecting the worst.

Her heart settled into the pit of her stomach.

There could only be one reason for Lydia to be so distraught. Had her uncle denied Lord Stanley permission to marry his daughter? Even worse, had Eleanor just committed the ultimate betrayal and made love to her cousin's future husband?

"Oh Eleanor, I'm so sorry. So, so sorry." Lydia grabbed her hand and dragged her into the drawing room. Then she closed the door so they could speak privately.

Eleanor's anxiety spiked at the action. "Did…" She could barely get the words out. She had to swallow before she could continue. "Did your father deny your request to break your betrothal? And what happened when Lord Stanley arrived?"

She never should have gone to see Geoffrey's sister. She should have stayed here today to see what would happen before setting plans into motion with her cousin's betrothed.

Lydia shook her head, her blond curls dancing about her face. "No, everything is fine with Lord Stanley. My father has agreed to end the betrothal."

The knot in her stomach began to ease. At least she wouldn't be living in a world where she would have to see the man she loved married to her beloved cousin. But her cousin's words made no sense. "Then what happened? Why are you so distraught? You should be happy."

The drawing room door opened, and Uncle walked into the room. "There you are, my dear. Has Lydia told you the good news yet? She's to be married to Lord Stanley."

"She did, Uncle, and I'm overjoyed for her. Lydia's happiness is very important to me."

Lydia grasped her hand and squeezed it as though she were trying to impart strength to Eleanor, which only added to her confusion.

"Well, now that Lydia's future is taken care of elsewhere, we still have the matter of Lord Hargrove to settle."

"I'm sure he will understand," Eleanor said, choosing her words carefully so as not to betray her personal interest in the man's future. "He is still young himself. I imagine he will have no difficulty in finding a countess."

The words were harder to say than Eleanor had expected. She only hoped she would never have to meet the woman who'd get to spend the rest of her life with the man that Eleanor loved.

Uncle shook his head. "Now that Lydia is to wed someone else, we must still secure a match between our two families."

"I don't understand," Eleanor said.

Her uncle's smile widened. "The agreement between the old earl and I can still be fulfilled if he marries you."

Eleanor's whole world turned upside down at those words. They made no sense. She turned to her cousin. "Did you know about this?"

Lydia shook her head. "Not until after Father accepted Lord Stanley's suit."

She turned back to her uncle. "I am of age, Uncle. You cannot force me to marry him."

Those words might have been the most difficult ones Eleanor had ever had to utter. She would love nothing more than to marry Geoffrey, but she couldn't force him into the union. He would hate her, and she couldn't live with that. It was far better to live with a broken heart than be hated by the man she loved.

CHAPTER 22

Geoffrey hadn't wanted to leave her, but he couldn't bring Eleanor home. He'd arranged for his carriage to take her home and then made his way to his house on foot. He was grinning like a fool the whole way.

He was surprised to find a note from Lord Appleby asking he call as soon as possible. He had a moment of worry, but he brushed it aside. Appleby wouldn't have requested his presence if he wanted the betrothal agreement to stand.

His first visit to Grosvenor Square at the beginning of the season had left him feeling frustrated. But today would put an end to the betrothal agreement. He didn't know if the solicitors would need to become involved, but after today he would be able to continue seeing Eleanor. He wouldn't have to worry that her guilt about betraying Lydia would put an end to their affair.

He was no innocent and had been with other women, but there was something unexpected about being with a woman you considered a friend. Someone he respected and admired for reasons that went beyond her beauty.

Eleanor had a quick mind and a kind heart, always willing to sacrifice her own desires so that her cousin would be happy. After today she wouldn't have to. She could be selfish, and he was the lucky man who would benefit from her exploration of what it was to be a woman. He very much looked forward to being her tutor on that journey.

He hated that at the age of twenty-five, she thought herself too old to capture a man's attention. She was just entering her prime and had a confidence and wisdom about her that was missing from the younger women who were newly out in society.

Thoughts of the pleasures they'd experienced that afternoon played in his mind as the carriage rattled over the cobblestones, and he tried to consider other reasons to excuse her absence from her uncle's town house in future. He couldn't expect his sister to act as a go-between even if she wasn't heavily pregnant with child. It was clear she hoped for more than a love affair between him and Eleanor, and he didn't want her to become disappointed in him. She'd already had far too many upsets in her life.

Would it be too conspicuous to increase their weekly visits to the bookstore? Ideally he'd like to see her daily, but he could only do that if he decided to make his interest in her known to her family. And once that happened, he suspected that Eleanor would no longer be free to meet with him at all. Her excursions would be monitored from that point on.

But perhaps, if Lydia and her mother were busy planning her wedding to Stanley, it wouldn't be too difficult for Eleanor to slip from the house and meet him more often. He was already beginning to feel anxious about when the two of them could be alone together again.

It occurred to him that he could marry Eleanor, but he shied away from that unexpected thought. He'd just gained his freedom. Did he want to turn around and bind himself to another woman?

But his heart told him that it wouldn't be just any woman. It would be Eleanor.

It was almost impossible to hold back his grin as the butler opened the door. He expected to be shown into Appleby's study again, where he'd met with Lydia's father to discuss the possibility of ending their betrothal. Instead, the butler informed him that they were expecting him in the drawing room.

His steps faltered when he found Appleby waiting, seated in an armchair, along with Eleanor. She was on the settee and was staring down at her hands. Surely this was a coincidence. Appleby couldn't have learned about their tryst that afternoon.

Pushing aside the thought, he entered the room and greeted the two occupants.

Lord Appleby stood and shook his hand. "Good, good. I'm glad you came straightaway. I'm afraid I have distressing news for you. But fear not, all is not lost."

He could feel Eleanor's eyes on him, but he kept his gaze fixed firmly on her uncle. He was so close to gaining his freedom. If Lord Appleby even suspected Geoffrey was taken with his niece, he could very well hide her away. Eleanor was under his protection after all.

Lord Appleby settled into his chair and waved him toward the other armchair. His gaze darted to Eleanor, and he saw she was staring at her hands again. He noticed then that they were gripped so tightly her knuckles were white.

He was struck with a premonition of doom. He wasn't going to be happy about the outcome of today's meeting.

"I came as soon as I got your message," he said. "You said it was very important."

Appleby nodded, steepling his fingers on his belly. "As you know, Lydia wanted to experience a full season unencumbered by any announcement of the betrothal agreement between the two of you. As a result, an unfortunate situation has arisen. I'm afraid that she's developed feelings for Lord Stanley. The man called today to ask for permission to marry her."

Geoffrey held back his grin of satisfaction. He'd been overreacting. Eleanor was here probably because Lydia had asked her to intercede on this matter. He'd begun to worry for no reason.

"I understand, and you already know my feelings on the matter. I don't want to force your daughter into an unhappy union when she cares for another. And Lord Stanley will one day be a marquess. You can hope for no better match for your daughter."

"Just so," Appleby said, his smile sympathetic. It was clear the man thought he was imparting disappointing news. "But there is still the matter of the property I sold to your father and the agreement we had in place."

Warning bells began to clang in his brain. "I don't know all the details, but I was recently made aware of the sale. But you should know that Stanley will one day possess vast holdings. Your daughter won't want for anything after they wed."

Lord Appleby's mouth tightened with displeasure. "It's a matter of honor. I sold those properties to your father with the express understanding that they would one day return to my family through marriage."

A frisson of alarm raced down his spine. "Are you telling me that you didn't accept Stanley's suit?"

"No, I did. Lydia will one day be the Marchioness of Pelton. But I am loath to lose those properties."

"I understand. I'll speak to my solicitor about reversing the sale. We can begin the process of returning those properties to you immediately."

Appleby scowled. "No, no, I don't want them back. That will leave more for my grasping cousin and his son to inherit."

Geoffrey said nothing as he examined the man. He could feel Eleanor's gaze on him again, but he didn't look at her. He wasn't going to like what came next.

"Did you examine the details of the agreement?"

Geoffrey nodded. "Of course. You need to understand that my father only told me about the betrothal on his deathbed. I feared he wasn't in his right mind at that point. I know he'd always hoped for a match between our families and thought that in the end he'd imagined a betrothal agreement that hadn't actually been signed. He was in a state of high fever when he told me."

Appleby shook his head. "I'm sorry to hear that. He was a good friend."

Geoffrey inclined his head but said nothing as he waited for the man to explain his cryptic comment.

"At any rate, the agreement does say that you were to marry my daughter."

Geoffrey nodded. "And you have just told me that you've accepted Lord Stanley's suit. And since the betrothal can be broken if both parties agree, I don't foresee any issues."

Appleby leaned forward in his seat. "I have a better idea, one that should suit both parties, as you say. I know you didn't wish to marry Lydia, although I can't imagine why. But the lands can remain in the family if you agree to marry my niece, Eleanor."

Geoffrey turned to look at her, but she was staring at her entwined fingers. Why wouldn't she look at him?

"I don't understand. There was nothing in the betrothal agreement about Miss Pearson."

Appleby shook his head. "I don't want the properties back. There is a clause in the sales contract that states if you don't marry Lydia, you are to marry my niece. I won't force Lydia to marry one man when she cares for another, but I do want that land to remain within my family." His jaw tightened. "Family that doesn't include my cousin, who will inherit my title and all the entailed properties."

Geoffrey's mind blanked for several moments,

and then images began to play over in his thoughts. The way Eleanor had approached him, telling him that she wished to engage in an affair with him. The way she'd so sweetly given up her innocence. Had she told her uncle what happened that afternoon between them?

No, he thought. Of course she hadn't. Appleby wouldn't be speaking to him in such civil tones if she had. He'd be demanding that Geoffrey do the honorable thing and marry his niece.

So Eleanor had kept their tryst to herself. But had she known about her uncle's plans when she'd approached him? Had she hoped that if they made love, he'd agree to marry her when her uncle spoke to him on the matter?

He rose to his feet, anger beginning to fill him. He'd been betrayed yet again. Manipulated into fulfilling Appleby's plans.

"I see," he said, somehow keeping his tone even. "Can I speak to Miss Pearson for a moment?"

Appleby frowned. "You don't need to worry about courting her, my boy. I've already informed her about her duty. But if you want some time to get to know her better—"

"When?" he asked through gritted teeth.

"When what? When will you marry? I thought perhaps after Lydia's marriage to Stanley."

"No. When did you inform her that it was her duty to marry me?"

Appleby stared at him as though Geoffrey had lost his mind. "Just this afternoon, when she returned from visiting your sister."

The tight band that had begun to constrict around his chest loosened the smallest fraction. Relief filled him at the knowledge that Eleanor hadn't been trying to trap him this afternoon.

"Can you allow us a few minutes to speak? It is clear to me that Miss Pearson is just as surprised by this turn of events as I am."

Appleby stood. "I understand, my boy. I don't know how well you've come to know her over the past weeks that she's been acting as Lydia's chaperone, but I can assure you that Eleanor is a lovely young woman, both inside and out. I'm sure she will make you very happy." He smiled at the two of them. "I'll allow you a few minutes to speak alone. My wife will join you after that. So if you want to begin your wooing, I suggest you act quickly."

He strode from the room, and for some time the only sound was that of his footsteps as he made his way down the hallway.

Geoffrey turned to look at Eleanor and only realized then that he was looming over her. He had the distinct impression that he was making her nervous. He wanted to sit next to her on the settee, but since he didn't know how soon Lady Appleby would arrive, he lowered himself into the armchair again.

He didn't know what to say. He'd been in such high spirits when he arrived, and now all his emotions were a confounding mess. But primary among them was anger at his father and Lord Appleby.

Eleanor finally met his gaze. "My aunt is quite busy making plans for Lydia's wedding, so I imagine she won't be here for some time. If you want to yell, rage, I quite understand."

How could she sound so calm?

Appleby had set his mind somewhat at ease, but he couldn't help but wonder if Eleanor had been aware this was a possible outcome when she approached him about having an affair. He was careful to keep his voice low when he asked, "Did you know about this when we were together this afternoon?"

Eleanor shook her head. "No, of course not. Uncle never spoke one word about this being a possibility. He was so determined that you were to marry Lydia. I first heard about this after I was home. Uncle had already sent his note asking you to call. I was trying to dissuade him from all this nonsense"—she waved her hands to encompass the space between them—"when you arrived."

His gaze remained fixed on her face. "What are you thinking?"

She raised her chin. "I am of age. Uncle can't force me to marry you."

His eyes narrowed. Did she need to say that as though the thought of marrying him was the worst fate that could befall her?

"From what he said, I'm sure Appleby would be most displeased. Would he cast you out?"

"I'll be fine as long as Lydia lives under this roof. And after…" She raised one shoulder. "Honestly, I don't think so. But if he did, I'm sure I could go live with Lydia. My cousin is quite generous."

He winced at the thought of her having to live under Stanley's charity. "I have houses. You wouldn't need to beg for somewhere to live."

She stiffened. "And what? You'll pay me an allowance and visit regularly to bed me?" She shook her head. "No."

She rose, and he did the same. "I'll wait a few

days before telling him that the two of us won't be marrying. I don't want to bring any negativity into the house when Lydia is so happy. But you needn't worry. I'll ensure my uncle knows that the two of us have decided there won't be a union."

Those were the words he'd wanted to hear all those months ago when he'd first set foot in this house. He would have his freedom and wouldn't be forced to wed. But he was no longer sure what he wanted.

"There is still some time before the end of the season. You don't need to say anything yet."

Eleanor shook her head. "I think it is best that we end things between us. The entire situation has become tangled beyond reason."

They stared at one another for some time. He took a step toward her, although he couldn't say why. She took a corresponding step away from him.

"It is probably best if you go now. We shouldn't be alone."

Geoffrey couldn't hold back his bitter chuckle. "Or they'll force us to wed. That seems to be my lot in life."

She winced at his words. "Thank you for discussing this matter with me and for understanding." Her gaze softened as she continued. "I enjoyed our time together very much. Thank you for showing me what might have been if things were different."

He began to reach for her, but she'd already turned and left the room. He stared at her departing figure, his soul bereft. Eleanor didn't want him.

CHAPTER 23

Geoffrey couldn't say why he set out for Holbrook's town house instead of returning to his own. Damn it all, the man had actually become a friend. He considered going to speak to his brother-in-law, but he knew Cranston already had enough on his mind and he didn't want to bother him further. Especially not when he and Abigail were trying to enjoy this time together, along with Gemma, as a family before Abigail's confinement.

They'd already imposed on his sister once today. Abigail had been only too happy to help him along with what she'd hoped would be a lasting relationship with Eleanor. He couldn't go there now without her wanting to hear how that was proceeding, and he didn't want to disappoint her. Not today when his own feelings were still raw.

When he arrived at Holbrook's, the man's butler asked him to wait in the drawing room, telling him that the viscount was expected home soon. He was pleased to find there was a sidebar stocked with liquor and helped himself to a drink. He'd just downed the brandy in one shot and was pouring another, determined to savor the second glass, when he heard the front door open and close.

He turned, glass in hand, and watched as his friend stepped into the room.

Holbrook raised a brow. "Were we supposed to meet today?"

Geoffrey shook his head and raised his glass. "I'm celebrating my freedom and wanted to share the news."

Holbrook settled into an armchair. "You brought Stanley up to scratch." He let out a low whistle. "I'm impressed."

Geoffrey sat in the other chair. He held on to the glass but didn't drink from it. He wasn't planning to become intoxicated, but he did want to numb some of his disappointment.

"There was very little effort needed on my part.

Once he saw Lydia and realized Appleby was intent on a match between her and me, Stanley took it upon himself to make Lydia fall in love with him." He took a swallow of the brandy and then placed it onto the side table with exaggerated care. "I wish the two of them every happiness."

Holbrook's eyes narrowed on him. "Then why am I sensing an air of melancholia about you? It's almost suffocating. I thought you'd be happier. Don't tell me you fell in love with the girl and now your heart is broken."

Geoffrey's mouth twisted at the very notion. "She's pleasant enough, but she's not the one for me."

"But her cousin is."

Geoffrey glared at Holbrook. "You see far too much."

Holbrook lifted one shoulder. "I'm observant. I assume you're here because you wish to speak to me about the other Miss Pearson."

It was a good thing he'd already put down the brandy. If he were still holding the glass, he would have tossed back the contents. "I've only just returned from calling on Appleby, who informed me that the betrothal would be broken."

"And?" Holbrook said when he paused.

"Apparently there's some property tied up between our two families, and Appleby insists that I marry Eleanor. He sold the property to my father with the intention that it would remain in the family. If I won't be marrying his daughter, he wants me to marry his niece."

Holbrook whistled. "You can't turn around without having women thrown at you."

Geoffrey scowled. "I'm glad you find my life so amusing."

Holbrook leaned back in his chair, his eyes narrowed. Geoffrey could feel the weight of the man's stare on him.

He was beginning to have second thoughts about coming here. He reached for the glass of brandy and finished the drink. But he wouldn't pour another.

Holbrook finally spoke. "I thought you liked the elder Miss Pearson?"

Liked was far too mild a word for what he felt for Eleanor. He longed to possess her in every way. After the afternoon they'd spent together, he'd thought his lust would've dimmed somewhat. But that hadn't happened. He'd been planning their next tryst as he said his goodbyes that afternoon, imagining all the things he wanted to do to her now that he no longer had to worry about her maidenhead.

"We are friends." He settled back in the chair and crossed his arms over his chest.

"Friends?" Holbrook raised one brow.

Geoffrey scowled. "I like her well enough and wanted to deepen that acquaintance now that she is free from any guilt she might feel about betraying her cousin. But I refuse to be led around by puppet strings and forced to do my father's bidding."

"Your father wanted you to marry Miss Lydia Pearson."

"I'm still being forced to wed."

"Are you?" Holbrook's tone was infuriatingly calm. "Is there something in the betrothal agreement that says you must marry the cousin?"

The two glasses of brandy were already dulling his thoughts. Geoffrey thought back over the conversation he'd had with Appleby. "No."

"And what does Miss Pearson have to say about this?"

Geoffrey let out a bark of laughter. "She thinks our acquaintance should become a thing of the past. She is of age, and while her uncle might desire the match, he can't force her to marry."

Holbrook smiled. "Then it appears that you've gotten everything you wanted."

No, damn it, he hadn't. He wanted Eleanor. But he resented being forced into marrying her. He closed his eyes and took several deep breaths. He tried to concentrate on the knowledge that in gaining his freedom, he would be thwarting his father's plans.

But all he could see was Eleanor's face as she ended things between them. He'd wanted to continue seeing her until the end of the season, but she'd refused.

"Since things are over between the two of you, I thought that perhaps I could befriend Miss Pearson. I've always found her intriguing."

Geoffrey's eyes snapped open, and his jaw clenched at the way Holbrook had said the word *befriend*. His hands clenched into fists on his knees, and he glared at the man who was supposed to be his friend.

Holbrook shrugged. "She's an attractive woman, and from what you've just shared, I won't need to worry about her trying to trap me into marrying her."

Geoffrey rose to his feet. "I forbid you from going near her."

A grin spread across Holbrook's face, and Geoffrey swore.

Holbrook stood. "We both know what's happening here. You want the woman for yourself, but you're being stubborn because you hate the idea of being forced to wed."

Geoffrey turned away. "That's not the issue."

Holbrook let out a derisive snort. "That is exactly the problem. You've spent your whole life hating everything about your father and what he expected of you. You had to watch him give your sister away in marriage to a man who was old enough to be her grandfather. My great-uncle wasn't kind to her, but I did what I could when I inherited the title. And she's happily married now. It all worked out in the end."

Geoffrey stiffened with each word, but he didn't interrupt.

"Your father wanted you to marry Lydia Pearson, and you did everything in your power to avoid giving him what he wanted even though he's no longer here. You've been blindly fighting against everything your father *might* have wanted even when it's what you *do* want. Why are you fighting so hard against the idea of marrying Eleanor? If you want her, go get her."

Holbrook's words lashed at him, but he couldn't deny they were true. He did want Eleanor. Why the hell was he fighting against this? He turned to look at his friend. "She doesn't want me."

Holbrook shook his head. "I've seen the way she looks at you. Trust me, that woman wants you."

Geoffrey remembered how she'd cried out his name when they made love. Their whispered promises about finding a way to meet more often. "She told me that we couldn't be together—"

"Because you've behaved as though you didn't want her or this marriage. Miss Pearson is not the type of woman who would force an unwanted marriage on another. She just spent the past few weeks watching you do everything in your power to get out of your betrothal agreement with her cousin. Do you really think she'd feel right forcing you to marry her? Of course she gave you your freedom. Because from everything you've told me, she'll always prioritize the happiness of those she cares about over her own."

The truth of his words struck him. "You're right."

"I'm always right. You need to let her know that you want her." Holbrook put his hands on Geoffrey's shoulders and actually shook him. "You want her, damn it. Go get her before someone else does."

Holbrook was right. He couldn't give her up. He'd been making plans to meet with her more often, to have her in his bed as often as they could manage it.

But beyond that, he wanted to hear her opinion on the latest book she was reading. It was more fun to hear her complaining about a simpering heroine than reading the book himself.

He'd been angry with Appleby. And for a brief moment he'd believed Eleanor had betrayed him. That she'd somehow seduced him to gain just this very end.

Which was a clear indication he was letting his anger about his father's scheming cloud his judgment because Eleanor wasn't manipulative. And the hurt he'd seen in her eyes…

He closed his own, a spasm of pain going through him. He loved her and couldn't lose her. And if that meant he had to marry her in order to have her, he would.

His decision made, he waited for the normal surge of anger that he felt whenever he was forced to fall in line with his father's wishes. But instead of anger, he felt anticipation at the thought of claiming the woman. He realized that he didn't *have* to marry her. He wanted to marry her.

He had to make things right with Eleanor.

CHAPTER 24

Geoffrey wanted to march straight to Grosvenor Square and speak to Eleanor, but he listened to Holbrook's advice to wait one day. Both he and Eleanor had already experienced a whirlwind of emotions today.

After a restless night's sleep, he rose early the next morning and scratched out a quick note. He imagined that it would be intercepted by Lady Appleby, so it was straight and to the point, stating simply that he intended to call that afternoon. It was returned several hours later unopened, the wax seal still in place.

He crumpled the note in his hand and glanced at the mantel clock in his study. It was early afternoon. He hadn't seen a wedding notice in the morning papers, which meant Appleby's town house would be filled with the usual hopefuls who were calling on Lydia.

He didn't want an audience for his discussion with Eleanor, and so he waited. Or rather he paced anxiously. Finally, when he deemed it would be safe, he set out. He should arrive just as the last of the callers were leaving.

When the butler showed him into the drawing room, he found Lady Appleby waiting for him.

"I wondered when you'd show up," she said, offering him her hand.

He bowed over it. "I'm sorry for arriving so late. But I wanted to speak privately with your niece."

She shook her head, not bothering to hide her displeasure as she sank onto the settee. "Eleanor isn't here."

He should have come here yesterday after leaving Holbrook's. "Where is she? When will she return?"

She stared at him for several long moments, a frown telling him she was displeased with him. He wanted to shake the information loose from her. Instead, he dropped into an armchair.

"You hurt my niece a great deal yesterday. I'm not sure she'll forgive you."

He stared at her for several seconds, taken aback by the accusation. But he couldn't deny he'd behaved petulantly. He wasn't shocked by her words so much as he was by the fact she'd spoken them about Eleanor. She'd always fluttered about Lydia, and he'd assumed she didn't really care about her niece's feelings. Appleby would have fretted about the land and expectations, but it seemed that his wife, at least, cared for Eleanor. And Lydia. It was clear she loved her cousin.

Still, he was long past making assumptions. If accusations were going to be made, then he'd give as good as he got.

Crossing his arms over his chest, he raised one brow. "Suddenly you care about Eleanor's feelings? I was under the impression you felt she existed solely to serve her cousin."

Lady Appleby had the good grace to flush. "I admit to being a little consumed about Lydia's season. But I can assure you that I love my niece very much. She has been an asset to her cousin this season, yes, but she also deserves to be happy."

He nodded. "I'm glad to hear that. I know that

she loves you all very much. Until this moment, I wasn't sure the feeling was mutual."

"Of course it is. Which is why I must ask how you intend to proceed. As Eleanor pointed out, we cannot force her to wed."

"Is that not what your husband tried to do when he told us that we needed to do our duty and fulfill the sale agreement that had been made between him and my father?"

"My husband can be shortsighted, and it appears that he made a muddle of things. It was I who broached the subject of a match between the two of you. He latched onto the idea and thought only of the precious land he'd sold. But Lydia told me that the three of you had spent a great deal of time together over the past few weeks. She came to me after Lord Stanley left here yesterday, but she said that she suspected there was something between the two of you."

The last statement surprised him. He'd always thought that Lydia was self-absorbed, but apparently she was more observant than he'd realized. "Your niece and I—"

Lady Appleby waved her hand, cutting off his protest. "I don't really care what happened or didn't happen between the two of you. I require no details. I know that Eleanor would never betray her cousin while the betrothal was in place, but Lydia told me that she allowed the two of you to wander off on occasion. That while you always seemed stiff and formal with my daughter, the same couldn't be said for how you behaved with Eleanor. Added to the fact that my niece always speaks highly of you…"

It was clear the woman wasn't finished with her little speech, so he remained silent.

Lady Appleby sighed. "I thought that proposing a marriage between the two of you would serve to make everyone happy. I don't know what you said to Eleanor when my husband allowed you some time together, but I can tell you she was very hurt. She tried to hide it behind happiness for her cousin, but a woman knows when another woman's heart has been broken."

The words struck him like a physical blow. "I need to speak to her. To apologize for my behavior."

She examined him before asking, "And that is all?"

There was no point hiding it now. Besides, the Applebys were Eleanor's family. It was only right that he let them know his intention. And he was finding it far easier to speak to Eleanor's aunt, who seemed genuinely concerned for her niece. "I've come to ask her to marry me. To beg her forgiveness for my stubborn behavior. She did nothing to deserve it, and I shouldn't have taken my annoyance with your husband out on her."

Lady Appleby gave him a sympathetic smile. "Oh, trust me, I've already given him a piece of my mind about how he mishandled the situation. But I must say, this is excellent news. It seems we're to have two weddings after all."

"Please tell me that she hasn't left London." It was his worst fear after learning she wasn't here. Would she have quit town to avoid him altogether? Did she hate him that much now?

Lady Appleby stared at him as though he'd lost his mind. "Of course not. Lydia has gone riding in Hyde Park with Lord Stanley. Eleanor is accompanying them as their chaperone. I offered to go in her stead, but she assured me she was looking forward to the fresh air."

She stood, and he came to his feet as well. "They left a short while ago. I'm sure you'll be able to find them there."

"Thank you for everything, my lady." He

dipped his head and then hurried from the house. He had a bride to catch.

He instructed the carriage driver to head toward Hyde Park. The trip was a short one, and he hoped luck would be on his side. It was still early, and if the park wasn't crowded, he might spot her faster from inside the carriage.

A few minutes later, he groaned when he saw the lineup of vehicles waiting to enter the park. He stopped the carriage and notified his driver to wait just outside the gates. He would have to search for Eleanor on foot.

He strode along the path, which was already filled with strolling couples and their chaperones. Lydia had wanted to walk that one time he'd brought her here, so he hoped they were on foot again. His heart had begun to race, but not from his quick pace.

He was forced to stop several times along the way when well-meaning acquaintances who thought he was in need of company tried to engage him in conversation. Finally, after twenty minutes that seemed much longer, he spotted them walking toward him. He froze in place and watched them.

They were walking as a group in the middle of the road. Lydia was holding on to Stanley's arm, her appearance that of a woman who wouldn't be able to walk without the support. The two had wide smiles and kept glancing at one another as though they were the only people present in the world. Really, it was a miracle they didn't trip over their own feet or bump into others who were walking in the opposite direction.

Eleanor was walking next to Lydia, and his heart broke as he stared at her. She kept glancing over at her cousin, and her expression was clearly pained. Since he knew she was genuinely happy for Lydia, Geoffrey could only attribute her sadness to him and the way he'd treated her.

He walked toward them. He was still several feet away when Eleanor must have sensed his presence because her eyes shifted to the left and unerringly met his. She stiffened and looked away again.

He wouldn't be deterred by her attempt to give him the cut. He deserved her censure.

Stanley called out to him when he reached the small group. Geoffrey greeted them and made a passing comment about the pleasant temperature.

A small frown formed between Stanley's brows. "I'm not sure whether you've heard—"

"I have," Geoffrey said, cutting him off. "I offer

you and Miss Pearson my sincerest wishes for a happy marriage."

Stanley's brow cleared. Then he looked around. "You're not here with anyone?"

His gaze was on Eleanor, who still wasn't looking at him. "Actually, I'm here for Miss Pearson."

Stanley opened his mouth to say something, but Lydia placed a hand on his forearm. "He means Eleanor."

"Oh right. Of course. You did mention what happened yesterday. But I was under the impression that matter was at an end."

Lydia was staring at Eleanor, and then she looked at him.

He wanted to grab hold of Eleanor's hand and drag her away somewhere private where he could beg her forgiveness. Instead, he said, "It is important that I speak to her. If you could spare her for a few minutes, I would be most obliged."

Lydia smiled, and he felt a shift in his chest. She knew he was here to make things right with her cousin.

"I don't think Lord Hargrove and I have anything to discuss," Eleanor said. "We settled matters yesterday, and I do not wish to revive the subject."

Stanley looked from him to Eleanor. "If Miss Pearson doesn't wish to speak to you…"

This time it was Lydia who cut him off. "Come, my love. We'll just walk on ahead for a little bit and give them a few minutes together."

CHAPTER 25

*E*leanor turned to Lydia, panic beginning to take hold. "This isn't necessary." The last thing she wanted to hear was another apology from this man. Or worse, he might hope to convince her to be his mistress.

Lydia smiled at her. "Just speak to him for a few minutes. You'll regret it if you don't give him this chance."

Eleanor gave her a tight nod but said nothing more. Lydia was in love and seeing romantic possibilities everywhere she looked. She wouldn't be able to convince her cousin that she was wrong.

Lydia reached out and grasped her hand. After squeezing her fingers, Lydia gave Geoffrey a sympathetic look, and then she and Stanley resumed their walk.

The man Eleanor had been hoping to avoid stepped into place next to her. He offered her his arm, but when she didn't take it, he clasped his hands behind his back. Without another word, they began to walk.

She was regretting her decision to accompany Lydia today. She'd gone to her bedroom yesterday after giving Geoffrey his freedom and asked for a dinner tray to be sent to her room. Her cousin had tried to convince her to join them that evening, but she'd been in no mood to go to yet another ball.

So today, when Lord Stanley had invited Lydia to visit Hyde Park, Eleanor had insisted on accompanying them. She'd had more than enough of crying over a man who didn't want her. It had been difficult, of course, watching Lydia and her betrothed together. It reminded her too much of the brief time she and Geoffrey had spent together yesterday afternoon.

How was it possible that only one day had passed since he'd shown her what might have been between them?

It had never occurred to her that she might see him here. At least he hadn't been with another woman. She wouldn't have been able to stop from bursting into tears if she'd seen another woman on his arm. She was barely holding her emotions in check now. He walked silently next to her, but his presence engulfed all her senses.

Tense seconds stretched to a full minute, and her nerves started to fray at the edges. Since it didn't seem that Lydia was going to return soon enough for her liking and put an end to this torture, Eleanor was going to have to do that herself.

"If you've come to apologize, you should know that isn't necessary. What my uncle tried to do was unacceptable."

"And apparently distasteful to you."

She chanced a quick glance at him and saw that he was frowning. She brought her gaze forward again. "My opinion and desires are of no conse-quence. You've made your distaste for the idea of marrying at this point in your life very clear. I understand why my uncle wanted to proceed with the arrangement, but what I said yesterday holds true. I won't force you to marry me, so you should consider yourself free."

She had to force the hated words out, but she couldn't quite keep her voice even. She just needed him to take his leave, and then she could begin working on regulating her breathing again.

"What if you wouldn't be forcing me?"

Was he trying to make this ordeal even worse? Or was it simply that he felt bad about how she must be feeling? He was a man of the world, and before yesterday she'd been inexperienced. Whatever the reason, she could no longer continue this conversation. "I think I should rejoin Lydia and Lord Stanley. Good day, my lord."

She quickened her step, but he stopped her, grasping her arm and turning her to face him.

Shocked, aware that they were beginning to attract attention, she glanced down at where he was holding her in place. Thankfully he dropped his hand.

She met his gaze again and swallowed, tears beginning to cloud her eyes. She couldn't let them fall, not here.

He swore under his breath when he saw them. "I was a fool, Eleanor. I lashed out yesterday because in that moment, when Appleby was making his decree, all I could see was my father and your uncle sitting together in a room, planning out my future. Coming to town at the beginning of the season and learning that I was betrothed..."

"I understand," she said. And she did. He hadn't known about the betrothal until his father was on his deathbed. Unlike Lydia, who'd known about the arrangement for years and had been willing to consider the match, it had been a complete shock to him.

"When I learned the truth, I felt trapped. And when your uncle told me that it was our duty to get married—"

"You felt trapped all over again, just when you'd finally achieved your freedom." She looked down, forcing herself to continue. "I do understand. Anything that happened between us was just a passing fancy on your part." She was rambling now, but she had to get all this out so it would finally be over. "We both know it was never going to last. You were always going to move on, and I'd be left with my memories. Perhaps one day I'll find someone who's content to have me as his bride…"

Gloved fingers came to her chin, and he tilted her face up to his. "No, Eleanor. I absolutely forbid you from accepting someone else's proposal of marriage."

Her thoughts blanked. What was he saying? "I don't understand. You forbid me?"

One corner of his mouth tilted up in a self-deprecating smile. "I can't have the woman I love and want to spend the rest of my life with agreeing to marry someone else."

She stared at him, unable to comprehend what he was saying. Finally she shook her head. "The woman you…"

She couldn't say the word. He'd spent the past few months trying to avoid romantic entanglements, so how was it possible that he could be telling her that he loved her… and here in Hyde Park where anyone could overhear them?

And then he dropped to one knee and reached for her hands.

Her mouth dropped open, shock going through her. "What are you doing?"

"Eleanor Pearson, would you do me the honor of becoming my wife? I find the idea of continuing without you unbearable, and I want the whole world to know that I love you."

If this was a dream, she never wanted to wake up. She smiled down at him. He loved her. He'd proposed in the middle of Hyde Park with half the ton watching them. "Are you certain?"

He looked around to where everyone else was now standing, not bothering to hide their fascination with the scene playing out in their midst. "Does it seem as though I'm uncertain?"

She shook her head in wonder. When she saw the slight vee forming between his brows, she rushed to reassure him. "I can't believe you're doing this here. Yes, my lord." She lowered her voice. "Yes, Geoffrey. I'll marry you."

Relief, affection, love, they were all present on his face as he rose to his feet. Then, uncaring about their rapt audience, he dragged her into his arms and kissed her.

She ignored the whispers that were beginning to reach her ears. Let the entire world talk about them.

EPILOGUE

June 1818

Two months had passed since that glorious day in Hyde Park. Eleanor had never thought it possible to be so happy. At times she thought she was in the midst of a dream from which she would soon wake up.

Her only frustration was that she and Geoffrey hadn't been able to make love again. Her aunt and uncle had increased their vigilance, making it impossible to find a moment alone together. She still saw him at the various balls and routs, and they all sat together in his theater box when they were watching a play.

Now that everyone knew about their upcoming

wedding, it was deemed acceptable for the two of them to share two dances. Even more interesting, other men who had never looked her way now took an interest in her. She couldn't say why, but Geoffrey insisted it was because she was no longer trying to hide.

She imagined they were just being polite, but their attention seemed to anger Geoffrey. So much so that he rarely left her side. His possessiveness was so contrary to how he'd been with Lydia while they were formally betrothed. Which was another bit of proof that he hadn't been tempted by her cousin.

There was still one month before their wedding, which was to be held just before the season ended. A double wedding with Lydia and Lord Stanley, at her cousin's insistence.

She stared down at the baby in her arms, Abigail and Lord Cranston's son. Gabriel was one month old today and was the most perfect child she'd ever seen. He had no hair, but his face was full, an adorable dimple in one cheek and the loveliest blue eyes. The same eyes he shared with his mother and his uncle.

Her heart was full to bursting at the knowledge that one day she could be holding their own child.

Geoffrey dropped a kiss on her cheek and then

held out his arms. "Abigail is going to take him away soon, and I'd like to hold my nephew."

She kissed Gabriel's bald head and then handed him over with a sigh.

Abigail sank down next to her on the settee and wrapped an arm about her waist. "It will be your turn soon."

They both watched Geoffrey, who settled into an armchair with the baby in his arms. He cooed down at his nephew, and Eleanor's heart clenched with longing.

Abigail's daughter Gemma, who was sitting on her other side, leaned against her and sighed. "All he does is eat and sleep. Papa says I must be patient and that soon I'll be able to play with him, but I'm not sure I believe him."

Eleanor laughed, joy filling her. This was exactly what she'd wanted and what she'd never thought to have. A family. Watching the way Geoffrey beamed with pride at the way his nephew gripped the finger he'd placed in his palm, she had the unerring certainty that he would make a wonderful father.

Their eyes met, and he must have realized exactly what she was thinking.

"Soon," he said, his voice filled with promise.

The next month couldn't pass fast enough for her liking.

Thank you for reading *Courting the Earl!* I hope you enjoyed reading Eleanor and Geoffrey's story. If you want more, there is a bonus epilogue available! Sign up for my newsletter at https://www.suzan namedeiros.com/newsletter to get access to my bonus content!

Holbrook's story is next in *Tempting the Viscount.*

Turn the page for an excerpt from *A Viscount for Christmas*, which is book 1 in my CHRISTMAS SCANDALS series.

EXCERPT—A VISCOUNT FOR CHRISTMAS

An unexpected Christmas gift…

When Viscount Isaac Thornton returns home for his mother's annual Christmas gathering, the last thing he expects to find is a beautiful woman sleeping in his bed. But Celia isn't yet another woman trying to trap him into marriage. She's his younger sister's best friend and now she's all grown up.

Celia Rowland outgrew the infatuation she had for Thornton years ago. When a misunderstanding means she's been compromised, her mother insists they get married.

One house party and two people trying to escape a forced wedding who just might get the Christmas gift they didn't know they wanted.

December 1816

It was past midnight when Viscount Isaac Thornton reached his estate in Surrey. He'd been on horseback for several hours. Normally the ride wasn't a difficult one, but with the cold temperatures, he'd needed to stop frequently to change horses.

Filled with a bone-deep fatigue that emphasized the unwelcome fact he'd recently passed his thirtieth birthday, all he wanted to do was sleep. He wasn't looking forward to the next week. His mother's yearly Christmas party would be yet another opportunity for her to remind him he needed to settle down and produce an heir. He couldn't avoid his mother's matchmaking altogether, but he could limit the duration of his suffering. Which was why he'd originally planned to arrive the day before Christmas and depart again the day after the holiday.

She'd successfully thwarted those plans with the greatest weapon in her arsenal—guilt. He'd received her letter that afternoon. In it, she told him how much she looked forward to spending quality time with him. She'd gone on to inform him that his two younger sisters, who lived in the north of England, wouldn't be attending because the roads were impassable after a heavy snowfall that hadn't reached Surrey. To alleviate what he knew would be her very real disappointment, he'd changed his plans and set out to join her when her house party would still be in full swing.

If he were being honest with himself, London had become tedious of late, especially after his friends and most of his acquaintances quit town and headed to their own estates for the holiday season. His mother's letter was a convenient excuse to return home earlier than planned.

He apologized to the sleepy groom who greeted him moments after he reached the stables. He was relieved to discover the manor was quiet as he made his way to the front door on foot. Perhaps his mother hadn't invited that many people this year.

But even as the thought occurred to him, he knew it was a futile wish. Christmas was his mother's favorite time of the year, and she was known for her winter house parties. This year wouldn't be any different.

He was surprised when the front door was opened by Saunders, their butler, and not a footman. He'd hoped to surprise his mother, but apparently she knew him too well. She'd expected him to set out for Surrey after receiving her letter.

He greeted the older man and handed him his hat and greatcoat, barely taking in the evergreen boughs and festive decorations that tastefully highlighted the fact the festive season was upon them. He'd started toward the stairs when Saunders coughed discreetly.

Thornton turned to face him.

"Your mother wishes to speak with you, my lord."

Thornton frowned. No doubt she wanted to tell him who she'd invited and why he should pay particular attention to each one of them. He'd just arrived, and already the matchmaking had begun.

He nodded. "I'll speak to her in the morning."

"She insisted—"

Thornton wouldn't take his annoyance out on this man whom he'd known since he was a child. Saunders was merely carrying out Lady Thornton's instructions.

"I already know what she wants to speak to me about."

"But—"

"Good night, Saunders. I'll speak to my mother first thing in the morning. And get some rest yourself." The man had no doubt been awake since dawn.

Before Saunders could say another word, Thornton turned and made his way upstairs.

He didn't ring for his valet when he reached his bedroom, too tired to care about the lecture the man would deliver tomorrow as he tossed his clothes onto a chair.

*-It was dark, but he didn't need to light a candle. He made his way to the bed and slid under the covers. His eyes were closing when a small movement on the other side of the bed chased away his fatigue.

He was imagining things. Or, more likely, he'd already fallen asleep and was dreaming. Still, he was wide awake now. He rolled over and narrowed his gaze on the other side of the bed, where he could see a small bundle wrapped in his blankets.

In retrospect, he should have sprung from the bed and thrown on his clothes. But he didn't really expect to find anything, and so he pulled back the bedsheets. It took his befuddled senses several seconds to process the fact he wasn't alone.

Someone was already asleep in his bed—a woman, to be precise. She lay with her back to him, and he could only stare at her for what felt like the longest minute of his life.

His fumbling in the dark hadn't caused her to move, so she must be asleep. His gaze took in the long golden hair that covered most of her back. Unbound, which surprised him. Unable to stop himself, he gazed down to where her hair ended just above the curve of her hip, which was covered in a white nightgown. The blankets covered the rest of her, and he resisted the temptation to drag them down even farther.

Casting aside the temptation to see whether she would be well endowed, he shifted onto his back and slung a hand over his eyes. He doubted very much that his mother had arranged this woman as a welcome-home present for him. She'd probably wanted to warn him that she had given away his room to another guest.

Which meant he had to dress again and find a servant to lead him to a room that was unoccupied.

He rose to a seating position with a muffled groan. He thought he'd been quiet, but the shifting of his weight must have woken the woman, because she rolled onto her back. Her eyes blinked open, and she let out a sleepy yawn. And then a scream.

That should have had him moving with alacrity, gathering up his clothes and escaping into the dressing room. But his brief glimpse at her form before she'd pulled up the bedcovers caused him to freeze. In the dim light, he could see that she was, indeed, well endowed.

Why did these things never happen to him under better circumstances? For it was clear now that he wasn't dreaming. If he were, she would have beckoned him to her with open arms. Instead, the woman in his bed had gathered up the blankets and held them to her breast like a shield.

"What are you doing here? You must leave at once!"

Yes, this wasn't a dream. "This is my bedroom."

Her mouth gaped open before she closed it with a snap. "You're not suggesting…" She took a deep breath and began again. "We can sort out this mess tomorrow morning. But a gentleman would leave without question and find another bedroom."

He couldn't resist teasing her. "Perhaps I'm not a gentleman."

She sputtered, speechless. Taking pity on her, he slipped from the bed with a soft curse.

"I don't know why you're upset. I'm the injured party here."

Something about the prim tone of her voice seemed familiar. He strode to the window and drew back the curtains to let in some of the moonlight. Then he returned to the bed—the side the woman occupied—and leaned forward to examine her. She leaned back with a squawk.

His eyes roamed over her face. Blond hair, blue eyes... she could have been anyone. But then he saw the small mole at the corner of her right eye.

"Celia Rowland?"

She huffed out an impatient breath. "That's Miss Rowland to you, my lord. Now will you please leave?"

He had to give her credit. Another woman might have given in to a fit of vapors at finding a man in her bed, but not Celia. He remembered her only as his youngest sister's friend. She'd been pretty, and he remembered finding her sweet, but she'd also been much too young for him the last time he'd seen her. He couldn't deny that she'd grown into a beautiful young woman.

He didn't miss the way her gaze dipped to his

bare chest and couldn't hold back his smirk. "Like what you see?"

Her eyes met his again. "I was merely—"

"Admiring my fine form? Wondering if you'd asked me to leave too soon?"

She let out an impatient huff. "Is it your intention to compromise me?"

And that's when the reality of the situation settled into place. His understanding came too late, however, because the bedroom door was thrown open.

BOOKS BY SUZANNA MEDEIROS

Dear Stranger

Forbidden in February

Anthologies:

The Novellas: A Collection

Hathaway Heirs: Books 1-4

Landing a Lord: Books 1-3

Landing a Lord series:

Dancing with the Duke

Loving the Marquess

Beguiling the Earl

The Unaffected Earl

The Unsuitable Duke

The Unexpected Marquess

The Unwilling Viscount

The Baron's Return

Courting the Earl

Tempting the Viscount (Coming Next!)

Christmas Scandals series:

A Viscount for Christmas

A Highwayman for Christmas

A Rogue for Christmas (Coming Next!)

Hathaway Heirs series:

Lady Hathaway's Proposal

Lord Hathaway's Bride

Captain Hathaway's Dilemma

Miss Hathaway's Wish

For more information and an up-to-date booklist please visit the author's website:

https://www.suzannamedeiros.com/books/

ABOUT SUZANNA

USA Today bestselling author Suzanna Medeiros was born and raised in Toronto, Canada. Her love for the written word led her to pursue a degree in English Literature from the University of Toronto. She went on to earn a Bachelor of Education degree but graduated at a time when no teaching jobs were available. After working at a number of interesting places, including a federal inquiry, a youth probation office, and the Office of the Fire Marshal of Ontario, she decided to pursue her first love—writing.

Suzanna is married to her own hero and is the proud mother of twin daughters. She is an avowed romantic who enjoys spending her days writing love stories.

She would like to thank her parents for showing her that love at first sight and happily ever after really do exist.

To learn about Suzanna Medeiros's future books (and to receive a bonus short story!) sign up for her newsletter: https://www.suzannamedeiros.com/newsletter

Visit her website: https://www.suzannamedeiros.com

Or visit her on Facebook: https://www.facebook.com/AuthorSuzannaMedeiros